Chronicles of Molly

Kerrigan Memoirs, Volume 4

W.J. May

Published by Dark Shadow Publishing, 2022.

CHRONICLES OF MOLLY

First edition. June 20, 2022.

Written by W.J. May.

Chronicles of MOLLY

USA Today Bestselling Author
W.J. MAY

Copyright 2022 by W.J. May

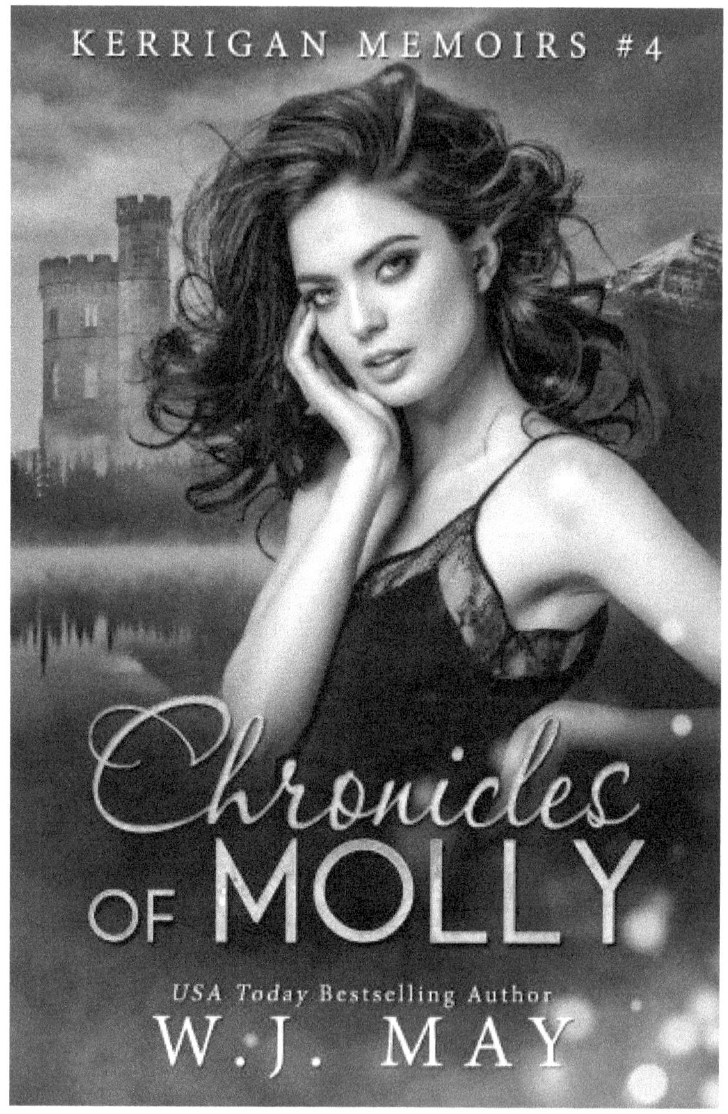
KERRIGAN MEMOIRS #4
Chronicles
OF MOLLY
USA Today Bestselling Author
W.J. MAY

THIS BOOK IS LICENSED for your personal enjoyment only. This e-book may not be re-sold or given away to other people. If you would like to share this book with another person, please purchase an additional copy for each recipient. If you're reading this book and did not purchase it, or it was not purchased for your use only, then please return to Smashwords.com and purchase your own copy. Thank you for respecting the hard work of the author.

Have You Read the C.o.K Series?

**The Prequel series is a Sub-Series of the Chronicles of Kerrigan.
The prequel on how Simon Kerrigan met Beth!!
Download for FREE:**

THE CHRONICLES OF KERRIGAN: PREQUEL –
Christmas Before the Magic
Question the Darkness
Into the Darkness
Fight the Darkness
Alone in the Darkness
Lost the Darkness

THE CHRONICLES OF KERRIGAN

Book I - *Rae of Hope* is **FREE!**
Book Trailer:
http://www.youtube.com/watch?v=gILAwXxx8MU
Book II - *Dark Nebula*
Book Trailer:
http://www.youtube.com/watch?v=Ca24STi_bFM
Book III - *House of Cards*
Book IV - *Royal Tea*
Book V - *Under Fire*
Book VI - *End in Sight*
Book VII – *Hidden Darkness*
Book VIII – *Twisted Together*
Book IX – *Mark of Fate*
Book X – *Strength & Power*
Book XI – *Last One Standing*
Book XII – *Rae of Light*

THE CHRONICLES OF KERRIGAN SEQUEL

Matter of Time
Time Piece
Second Chance
Glitch in Time
Our Time
Precious Time

The Chronicles of Kerrigan: Gabriel

Living in the Past

Present for Today

Staring at the Future

Kerrigan Chronicles

Book 1 – Stopping Time
Book 2 – A Passage of Time
Book 3 – Ticking Clock
Book 4 – Just in Time
Book 5 – Time in the City
Book 6 – Ultimate Future

The Kerrigan Kids Series

Book 1 - School of Potential
Book 2 - Myths & Magic
Book 3 - Kith & Kin
Book 4 - Playing With Power
Book 5 - Line of Ancestry
Book 6 - Descent of Hope
Book 7 – Illusion of Shadows
Book 8 – Frozen by the Future
Book 9 – Guilt of My Past
Book 10 – Demise of Magic

Book 11- Rise of the Prophecy
Book 12 – Deafened by the Past

Find W.J. May

Website:

https://www.wjmaybooks.com

Facebook:

https://www.facebook.com/pages/Author-WJ-May-FAN-PAGE/
141170442608149

Newsletter:

SIGN UP FOR W.J. May's Newsletter to find out about new releases, updates, cover reveals and even freebies!

http://www.wjmaybooks.com/subscribe

Chronicles of Molly

THE PROVERBS SAY THAT absence makes the heart grow fonder. **But sometimes the proverbs get it wrong.**

Molly Skye has the life she always dreamed of. A ritzy penthouse in the city. A child she adores. A best friend to share in all her magical adventures, and a gorgeous husband waiting in her bed.

But the problem with dreams, is they vanish when it's time to wake up.

When Molly gets an urgent call from her mother, she's forced to return to the family home relocated in Scotland. But things have never been easy between the two women, and when tensions erupt between them, it's unlikely the little rural town will ever be the same.

A surprise visitor arrives to the cool those fiery tempers, but when a massive prison break shakes the foundations of the Privy Council, all bets are off. The friends make plans to race back to London, only to discover they aren't the only ones in Scotland and that trouble has already arrived.

What happens when the old world collides with the new? When the dust finally settles, will there be anything that survives? Maybe those proverbs got one thing right after all.

One way or another...there's no place like home.

Chapter 1

"Molly Elizabeth...Fodder."

The girl perched on a chair in front of the vanity, studying her reflection with a curious expression, like she was trying it on for size. Long ripples of crimson hair cascaded down her back, and despite the fact that she wasn't wearing anything more than a bathrobe, her tiny feet had been strapped into a pair of lethal stilettos. She rested her chin upon her hands, letting out a quiet sigh.

There was a stack of papers on the desk behind her—the stuff she usually avoided. Intake forms and other logistics. They had all been completed. But the line at the top was left blank.

Molly Elizabeth...?

The door opened and shut behind her. Despite all her training, despite the fact that she was sitting in front of a mirror, she didn't notice. Her bright eyes had glassed over, and her gaze was fixed in the middle distance. The delicate point of her chin was imprinted into her hand.

"Nice legs."

She whipped around, then lowered her gaze.

If she hadn't spent the last few years living in the firm grip of the surreal and fantastical, she might have second-guessed her own ears. If she hadn't spent the last few years raising a now seven-year-old boy, she might have wondered how a talking robot had found its way into her room.

She leaned closer, hands on her knees. "Excuse me?"

It stared back without expression, dented along the brow where Benji had used it as a shovel in an attempt to tunnel into the neighbor's backyard. The mouth glowed and it creaked up a hand.

"Take it off."

...my leg?

She lifted her eyebrows slowly and the robot glitched, like something had struck it across the face. A second later, it tried again, lowering those mechanical eyes to look her up and down.

"Your clothes," it corrected. "Take off your clothes."

What in the world?

Those years of training had given an edge to all her natural instincts, and a voice piped up in the back of her mind advising that this aluminum nightmare was most likely winding up to kill her.

But a rising suspicion quelled those dangerous thoughts, curving her lips with a smile. She pushed up from the chair and bent over so they were the same height, hands on her knees.

"You want me to take off my clothes?" she repeated lightly. "Is that what you dream about at night, you little creep? When we plug you into the wall to recharge?"

The robot had been a necessary incursion into the already impossible chaos of the happy little house. When a boy at Benji's school had brought one for show-and-tell, he'd embarked upon an Irish hunger-strike until he'd gotten one for himself. After the second day finding him swaying dizzily in the confines of his closet, his parents had capitulated and ordered one of the approximate size and color. It was a decision they'd bitterly regretted almost every day since.

Her question went unanswered, as the robot stood before her with a blank stare. For a split second, she was convinced it had lost power. Then it capsized in a bizarre curtsy.

"Fair maiden," it responded in a flat-monotone, "tell me of your dreams." There was a pause as those yellow eyes fixed upon her face. "Or maybe you want music-time?"

The robot then attempted to dance.

I can't un-see this...

She watched a few seconds, armed with the dreadful knowledge that this would most likely *not* be the strangest part of her day. Then it lifted its arms with a final instruction.

"Applause."

That's it.

Without another word, she stepped over the tiny machine and out into the hallway, taking only a moment to gauge her options, before yanking open the closet to find her husband kneeling on the floor. His head whipped up in alarm, and he hastened to hide the remote he'd been holding behind his back. When she reached for the tiny camera, he panicked and shoved it into his mouth.

She folded her arms slowly, flashing a dangerous smile. "Honey, you wouldn't happen to know anything about a pervy robot hitting on me, would you?"

Demanding amputations and stripping.

"Some pervy robot is hitting on you?" he exclaimed, leaping to his feet and moving slight back, away from the camera. "I'll kick its arse!" He raised both fists, before flashing the world's most adorable smile. "Unless...you wanted music-time... with me, after all?" He lifted his eyebrows invitingly, swaying his hips in an absurd approximation of whatever dance the robot had been attempting to do itself. "We could always keep that option open—"

She jumped into his arms.

"How are you so freaking cute?" she demanded, kissing him wildly and wrapping her legs around his waist. "And weird, Luke! You're SO freaking weird!"

He let out a breathless laugh, anchoring a hand behind her head, while kicking the door shut behind them. The closet wasn't incredibly spacious, it was used mostly for storing extra winter clothes and linens, but they'd repurposed it for this sort of thing before. They had regular grips for balance, regular places to wedge their feet. They'd gotten it down to a science, except—

"Ow!" Luke jerked back suddenly as the heel of her stiletto dug into his leg. "Why in the world are you wearing those? Didn't you just get out of the shower?"

She glanced down with a flush, having forgotten all about them, then lifted her leg with a mischievous smile—notching one of those lethal points behind his neck. "What...*these*?"

He caught his breath, running his fingers down the length of her leg. "I'll never understand how you can stretch like that—"

"Spy school," she interrupted flatly, staring at him all the while. "I enrolled in spy school, just to learn how to stretch like that. They taught me all sorts of tricks, gave me all sorts of *cars*..."

His eyes twinkled with silent laughter.

"Don't," he warned, biting playfully at her neck. "You know I can't talk about cars when we're like this. It's overwhelming, I start to get faint..."

She did know. Last year at Christmas, she'd taken a picture of herself in her birthday suit, lying atop the hood of his favorite convertible, and slipped it into his stocking. He'd taken a single look, crossed himself, then vanished to 'check on the air filters.' He hadn't returned for a long time.

"I just can't stop thinking about them," she whispered into his ear, slipping her fingers into the top of his pants. "The twin-turbo engines, the superchargers, the ignition control..."

He leaned back suddenly, looking profoundly touched. "Honey, did you learn all those things for me?"

Her eyes danced with mischief. "Oh, I've learned all sorts of things for you. Come here"—she pulled him a back again, biting his lower lip—"let me show you—"

The closet door flew open.

"There's something wrong with my robot!"

The couple detached with a gasp, frantically pulling their clothes back together, as a furious red-haired boy glowered in the hall. He'd never understood why his parents sometimes disappeared into the closet. He wondered if they were checking for mice and ventured in by himself on occasion, looking for the same. But such curiosities were no longer of concern. The child had been sabotaged.

"Benji, can you just—" Luke raked back his hair, trying desperately to re-button the top of his pants. "Can you just wait in the living room? I'll be there in a second—"

"It's *angry* with me!" the boy interrupted, thrusting the robot between them. "When I tried to feed it breakfast, it told me to take off my ears!"

There was a pause.

"I'm sure it's a misunderstanding."

"Why were you feeding it breakfast?"

There were a few seconds of silence, wherein each of them replayed the last few sentences and the boy worried that he might have overplayed his hand. He shot a bracing look at his parents, still lodged awkwardly amidst the spare bedding, before bolting full-speed for the kitchen, sensing that if he didn't manage to feed the robot now, he might never get a chance again.

The couple shared a panicked look, then scrambled after him.

"Benji, you get back here..." Molly trailed off in horror, sliding to a stop on the marble floor.

It had only been a few minutes that the child had been left unattended. Only a few minutes, yet the house had been transformed. Ribbons of toilet paper had been strung like garlands from the chandelier. A herd of dinosaurs had taken up residence upon the couch. There was a potted plant on the kitchen counter that she had never seen before, while the toaster was full of—

"Is that shaving cream?"

She reached out a tentative finger, and Benji let out a plaintive wail.

"It's lava for my ice-monsters! Don't touch it!"

Her eyes lifted slowly, falling on the interrogation chamber just beyond. At one end of the kitchen hung a noose made of designer neckties. Beside it lay a plate of untouched biscuits.

It seemed the robot had been given a choice.

"Benji, what did I tell you about putting magnets on the..." Luke trailed into silence, his bright eyes sweeping around the house. "...elevator."

It had been a difficult adjustment, moving from the sparseness of a sixteenth century monastery, into the whimsical decadence of his wife's penthouse. The walls had been covered in gilded mirrors and paintings. His clothes had been relocated to the attic to make room for her shoes.

It had been another adjustment when they'd had a child. Those same shoes were often covered in stickers. Everything else had been moved above the reach of seven-year-old hands.

A shock to the system, yet he was often called upon to be the voice of 'reason' in the house, to rein in his high-spirited, fire-haired family and provide a dose of sanity to keep things afloat.

"Lucas...do something."

After triaging in terms of urgency, he paced toward the kitchen and unplugged the toaster from the wall. Then he dipped his fingers into the cream...and smashed it into his wife's face.

"What?!"

On second thought, he'd never been too reasonable himself.

There was a burst of lightning, then she was upon him—swinging from the noose for leverage, before rocketing into his arms. He caught her with a burst of laughter, and staggered backward into the microwave. The chandelier swayed precariously above them, but didn't fall.

"I'm going to *kill* you, do you know that?!" she shrieked, scooping the foam off her cheeks and smearing it violently over his own. "I'm going to actually *kill* you this time!"

With a feral battle cry, Benji threw himself into the fray—still gripping the malfunctioning robot, which had started dancing once again. Its yellow eyes flickered ominously and its limbs creaked in protest as each of the little family made a desperate grab for it at the same time.

The residents below lifted their eyes to the ceiling, as three voices echoed from above.

"No cyborgs in the house!"

"Is that a noose?!"

"Deploy the laser!"

Molly and Luke paused in unison, throwing a panicked glance at their son, half-convinced some unearthly burst of light would shoot forth and roast them all to bits. The boy let them hang a moment, let them lean closer, then spat out a mouth of shaving cream with a vengeful cry.

"You'll never take us alive!"

There were squeals of laughter and shrieks of rage, as the trio collectively slipped on the slick marble and tumbled onto the floor. At that point, Molly secured a grip on the robot and tossed it into the fireplace with a triumphant cry, as the boys located the rest of the shaving cream and took up defensive positions on opposite sides of the room. The tables shifted quickly, as was so often the case in tales of urban guerilla warfare, and she ducked hastily behind the counter.

There was a vibration in her pocket.

She answered without looking. "Rae?" she panted breathlessly. "Unless you want to fly over with a few of those percussion grenades we stole from that munitions dump, it's not really a good—"

"Molly, it's your dad."

She detached herself from the fight immediately, ducking a glob of shaving cream and pressing a hand over her ear. "Dad? I can hardly hear you. Is everything okay?"

The lights flickered precariously, as his voice crackled from a country away.

"Hang on, can you—" She waved a paper towel above the counter, praying for a moment of peace. It was quickly covered in shaving cream as well. "Can you say that again?"

A throat cleared through the static.

"I said that I need you to come home, sweetie. Your mother needs someone in the house while she's recovering from surgery, and I'm going to be lambing with your uncle until May."

She froze a suspended moment, unable to decide which part of the sentence to tackle first.

"Surgery?" she repeated incredulously. "What are you talking about? When in the world did Mom have—*enough with the shaving cream*!"

There was a pause in the battle, as two heads peeked up from behind the couch.

"She had a knee replacement five days ago," he answered mildly. There was a creak of old leather, as he stretched back in his favorite chair. "It went fine, she's home now."

Molly's lips parted in delayed shock. "Why didn't you tell me?"

There was an awkward pause.

"You know your mother...she didn't want to make a fuss."

She didn't want me to know.

She was standing by now, and the others had clearly realized from her tone that something serious was wrong. Luke emerged slowly from amidst of barricade of throw pillows. Benji was hanging from his neck like a backpack. Both were eyeing her with the same look of concern.

The second part of the sentence was sinking in.

"Well...why can't you stay with her?" she asked with a flicker of panic, fingers tightening like a claw around the phone. "This is medical, what could possibly—"

"I told you," he interrupted patiently. "I promised your uncle Charlie I'd help with the lambing this season. Todd and Malcom are both off at school, the poor man's overwhelmed."

She flashed a quick look at the phone, then covered the receiver. "Dad, you're over sixty and you don't have a beard. How is it *possible* that you think lamb is a verb?"

"Come now, girlie. You know how this goes." He leaned back again, a thick Welsh accent leaking through. "Someone needs to guide the poor creatures. There are lanterns to be lit, stables to be mucked. Your mother is safe in the village, the ewes are scattered across the windswept moor!"

"Scattered across the windswept moor..." Molly repeated slowly, rubbing her eyes. "Why do all of our conversations make me feel like I've strayed into a Jack London novel?" She'd grown up in Wales and at one point in Guilder, her folks had picked up and moved to Scotland. She sometimes wondered how her dad had managed to keep his Welsh accent and mixed in Scottish dialect without creating an entire new language.

"Now wait just a minute—"

"Why can't Luke go lambing for you?" she interrupted with a touch of desperation, careful to avoid her husband's gaze. "You remember last time...he loved Uncle Charlie."

Luke shook his head quickly, remembering as well.

The chair had stopped creaking, her father was sitting up now. Just like her husband, he had often been called upon to provide the balance between two such tempestuous women, a pillar of stability when those clashing natures threatened to destabilize all the rest.

Most days, this meant creating a healthy bit of distance.

But sometimes, they needed a little push.

"Molly Elizabeth. You need to come home."

Her heart sank and her shoulders wilted with a sigh. "Yeah, of course. I'll just...I'll figure it out. Call you soon, okay?"

The line went dead and her arm drifted down to her side. At the same time, Benji took it upon himself to deploy the last of the shaving cream, flinging a giant dollop right into her face.

Her eyes snapped shut, as it slid down her nose.

I am home.

LESS THAN AN HOUR LATER, the situation was already starting to improve.

After making her way hastily through the five stages of grief—lingering perhaps longer than was healthy on bargaining—Molly found a solution to her problem by merely shifting the blame.

She could not *possibly* go to Scotland. Not when she was needed right there.

"Alright, Mommy loves you so much, *so* much." She planted a kiss on Benji's forehead. "But I'm about to electrocute you for the shaving cream, and your grandpa just called up and made some serious threats. So Auntie Angel's going to watch you for a few hours, while Mommy goes to work."

He eyed her speculatively, standing on the curb. "Do you think she'll play warrior with me?"

There was a pause.

Babysitting with Angel was always a mixed bag.

On the one hand, the children absolutely adored her, but after a particularly rough afternoon, Molly had once returned to find them all frozen like Medusa's statues in the backyard.

"Aunt Angel does that a little differently than the rest of us. But if you present her with a roving target and offer a bribe to the wolf, there's a good chance you'll survive until dinner."

She smacked a final kiss on his cheek and sent him running into the house before turning on her heel and waltzing off toward the blazing red convertible parked just up the street.

While she and the others might have delighted in teasing the men for their obsession, she appreciated the feel of Italian chrome just as much as the next girl, especially when it matched the precise shade of both her lipstick and hair. She slid inside and fired up the engine—shooting off down the road toward the magical solution to all her mundane problems.

It was an hour drive outside London. She made it in thirty minutes.

The school was busy at the time she arrived—the bells in the great tower had rung and the students were hurrying to find seats in their next class. It seemed like another lifetime that she'd been one of them—flipping her hair and giggling with Rae, casting secret looks at the boys.

They'd always been certain of their future, in the same way that every teenager gifted with superpowers was inexplicably sure of what would come next. They would be heroes, that much was inevitable. They would rise to uncharted new heights and probably save the world a few times along the way. Their legends were already spinning themselves by the time that magical ink settled upon their skin. They were already making promises, making plans.

They could never have imagined how those plans would change along the way.

"Good morning, Ms. Skye!"

Molly startled from her thoughts and lifted a belated hand, waving to a cluster of freshman a second too late. In the beginning, they'd been too nervous to actually speak with her. It was even worse when she was with Rae. Ink was like currency in a place like Guilder, and her gang of friends had managed to spin a great many of those legends after all. They were revered amongst their peer group, the younger generation openly worshiped at their feet. It was a little isolating, to be perfectly honest. But when Luke had started teaching at the school, that exclusivity had begun to chip away.

Speaking of my absent husband...

With the threat of 'lambing with Uncle Charlie' hanging over his head, Luke had gotten dressed much faster than usual that morning and fled to the school—quite possibly before he could be conscripted into any familial obligations that left him stranded on the Scottish Highlands. He was teaching now—something that had started as an experiment and grown into a passion.

He seemed almost too young for it, but that was part of the appeal. There was something irresistible about having a teacher with scars from his own missions. A teacher with rebellious hair, and an irresponsible car, who'd spent a great deal of his adolescence working for the 'other side.'

It had bridged the gap between them, created friends, where before there had been only fans. There had been many occasions when one of those students would turn up in his office on campus, or even at their own dinner table at home. Sometimes they would talk—a great and sudden outpouring, as if they'd only needed someone to listen. Sometimes they would listen themselves.

Molly was often uncertain in those times. Ruled by emotion and practiced only in dealing with those under the age of ten, she rushed to fill any silence and move them from one moment to the next. Luke was more patient, more constant, with a unique understanding of what that precise person needed in that *precise* moment of time. It was one of the things she loved most about him.

There were few things that made her prouder than watching her husband pace in front of a captive audience, lecturing with that earnest charisma that had students hanging onto his every word.

There were few things more rewarding to sabotage whenever she was on campus herself.

With a secret grin, she ghosted across the grass toward the history building, weaving through the hedges before tapping enthusiastically on the glass. A dozen pairs of eyes turned in unison as she began waving and blowing extravagant kisses. Luke glanced up from his notes, then blushed and covered his face while his students started laughing uproariously in the background.

The lesson was forgotten. The teasing was underway.

My work here is finished.

Feeling immensely pleased with herself, she skipped back across the grass and headed into the Oratory, pushing open the heavy double doors with a mighty shove. There were a dozen people scattered across the mats, less than usual. She latched quickly upon a familiar face.

"Hey you!"

Devon was standing between the weapons bin and the mannequins they used as targets, a bunch of discarded spears gathered at his feet. Instead of picking them up, he was stretching out his arms with a little wince, twisting slightly to loosen the muscles around his shoulder blades.

"Hey," he murmured, focused on the task.

She pulled up short, looking him over in surprise. "Are you okay?"

He nodded distractedly, raking back his dark hair.

"I think so," he answered without really thinking, testing the limits of each arm. "Last night, Rae and I were trying this—" He glanced up suddenly, like he'd just fully registered he was speaking to another person. "I was just...sparring," he concluded rather lamely. "I hurt myself sparring."

Molly folded her arms with a wicked smile. "Sparring, huh?" she repeated. "So was this with Rae? Or Julian?"

His eyes narrowed ever so slightly. "Rae."

She lifted her hands innocently. "Just checking—you were *sparring*, after all. Could have been with anyone."

The jokes were unending and she likely could have continued amusing herself for quite some time, but her eyes softened with pity when he winced again. With a regretful sigh, she reached into her purse and pulled out a bottle of over-the-counter pain meds, tipping two pills into his hand.

He glanced up in surprise, then flashed a little grin. "You are such a mom."

She unscrewed a bottle of water, lifting it to his lips. "Drink."

He took an obedient swig, grinning again when she cupped a hand beneath his chin.

"You should really get Alicia to heal that for you," she advised, tossing the bottle back into her purse. "Since you're apparently too chicken to talk to your wife."

He shook his head, bouncing a little to loosen up. "I went to Aly with something like this a few weeks ago, and she was super weird about it." He lowered his voice conspiratorially, flashing a sudden look around the mats. "I think she gets a lot of this kind of stuff."

Hazards of working at a supernatural school.

Molly snorted with laughter. "Hang in there, Dev. It gets better." She clapped him cheerfully on the same arm and skipped off down the hall. "On second thought—train harder. It might help you keep up."

He attempted a rude gesture, then winced again.

My work here is finished as well.

With a satisfied grin, she pressed the 'secret' lever in the Oratory wall and stepped back as the smooth paneling slid open to reveal a staircase that led to the lower tunnels.

The first time she'd seen that happen, she remembered gawking in wonder, then pushing Rae through the door first—just in case. The first time her son had seen it, he'd planted himself in front of the lever like some kind of troll and attempted to charge the agents for safe passage.

To each their own.

She hardly noticed it now.

Her fingers drummed impatiently on her sweater before they glided to a stop and she swept down the stairs—flashing a polite smile at a lone bison who was attempting the drinking fountain.

Before Carter had assumed the presidency of the Privy Council, the tunnels and everything inside them had been the worst kept secret the supernatural community had to its name. This was from a group of people who'd once rolled down the curtains at an alumni dinner, in the vague hope the students wouldn't see the supersonic jet taking off beneath the trees. In the subsequent years since his promotion, those rigid boundaries had slackened significantly—yielding to allow a wider group of people inside. The sacred halls of Guilder were no longer a sanctuary for emancipated teenagers—mourning the loss of their previous family, whilst simultaneously embracing the wonders and responsibilities of ink. They became a rallying point for entire generations. Doors opened and secrecy vanished. Entire families—whether or not they carried a tatù—were welcomed into the fold.

The structure itself had changed to reflect the new spirit.

Dormitories had been expanded to allow for siblings, the corridors were no longer barren, but framed in pictures and memorials—a sea of smiling faces stretching down the length of the halls. Upon the fierce insistence of some of its more valued agents, a daycare had even been added beside the research wing. An unprecedented request, but the friends themselves had led the charge, refusing to work until they had "the same benefits as someone working at Home Depot."

It helped a great deal that Carter happened to be a grandfather.

It helped even more that Angel had been providing tactical support.

These days, the policy was rather simple: as long as you carried the secret, not just the ink, the doors of Guilder University would be open to you.

Those boundaries were carefully monitored, of course. With the help of nmenokinetics like Natasha, an ever-present team of people were keeping track of such things every day. But there wasn't a single person—either in the agency, or at the school—who wouldn't say it was worth the extra risk. If ever one started to worry or doubt, they had only to look out the window at the sea of happy, blended faces to find themselves convinced.

Magic brought people together. It no longer drove them apart.

In theory...

Molly breezed quickly down the hallway to the large office at the end. It was mostly avoided by the other agents, the way people tended to give space to the cave of a sleeping bear. But since each of them had turned sixteen, she and her friends had taken to haunting the place whenever possible.

She scarcely knocked before cracking the door open. "Hi there, do you have a second?"

Carter looked up from a mountain of paperwork, beckoning her forward with a welcoming smile. "Of course. Anything to delay the inevitable."

She cocked a finger toward the bison in the hallway. "You know Craig is messing with the faucets again?"

He took off his glasses and rubbed his eyes. "I can't tell you how many times I've told him not to do that," he muttered, looking utterly exhausted. "The man's as impervious to disciplinary action as the lot of you."

That can't be right.

She slipped inside the office and settled into a chair. "We could find him a pasture, set him out to graze."

Carter chuckled and slid the glasses back onto his nose. "What can I do for you, Ms. Skye?"

Here goes nothing.

"I got a call this morning from my dad," she began tentatively. "Apparently my mom just got a knee replacement, and he's asking that I come to Scotland for a few days to help with the recovery."

In a flash, Carter's expression transformed. "Oh, I'm so sorry to hear that!" he exclaimed, rearranging a dozen international logistics on the fly. "Well, of course you're welcome to—"

"I'm staying in London."

"—take as much time as you need."

There was an awkward pause.

"Alright…" He leaned back with a slight frown, trying to interpret her expression. "I feel like I might be missing something. You didn't come here requesting a leave of absence? You don't want to spend some time in Scotland with your mother?"

She froze a split second, regarding him across the desk.

He's not making a joke. He's never met her.

"It's not that I don't want to," she began innocently, "it's just…it's just impossible right now with work. That's why I'm here. I was hoping maybe you could sign something to that effect."

And now that I'm saying it aloud, I sound about six years old.

Carter stared a moment longer, then nodded slowly. "I see," he murmured, lowering his gaze and needlessly straightening the papers littered across his desk. "Molly, this may be a personal question, and I don't mean to pry, but would you like me to send a healer? That way, there's no need for recovery at all."

He hesitated a moment, treading lightly. "I only ask because I've never met your mother."

It was a delicate way of asking a delicate question.

When the doors of Guilder had opened, the campus had been swarmed and the man had been inundated with more faces than he could possibly match to names. People from all over the country, from all over the globe, had flooded the English countryside, desperate to see the mythical school that had kept their sisters, or brothers, or cousins away from them so long.

Carter had received each and every one. He'd shared stories, and shared meals. He'd listened to the concern of parents, to the intense jealousy of siblings, to the outright disbelief and wonder, and also the anger of having been kept so long at bay. He'd done it all, and they'd grown stronger for it.

But there were a few notable faces missing from the crowd.

When the doors of Guilder had opened, Eleanor Skye had moved to Scotland and pretended her daughter was away at boarding school in the Alps.

I could probably write that note for him myself.

Their eyes met for a split second, then Molly looked away.

"Haven't you?" she said lightly, static crackling in her palms. "No, I guess not. She's been really busy these last few years. First, there was the move to Scotland, then they had to settle into the house. Then she redecorated the house a couple of times."

Carter nodded silently, gazing with a thoughtful expression at his desk.

"Anyway, I don't have anything set up in terms of lunches for Benji. And I'd miss the fiftieth day of his spring semester. Suppose that makes me a bad mother."

There was another excruciating silence.

"Then of course, there are the logistics to consider. The woman knows I fear nature, so she decided to move to the middle of nowhere in Scotland. The town doesn't even have a Starbucks, and the grocery store is nothing more than a glorified barn. Even if I could manage to stock up on enough allergy medication to survive it, there's still the fact that I'd be trapped there alone with my—"

She caught herself quickly, flashing him a quick glance.

"The thing is, you never know when I might be called upon to save the world," she finished with the hint of a plea. "Remember how many times I've done that already—"

Carter stood up slowly, gazing down with a gentle smile. "Molly...go home."

She went pale as a corpse.

"Pack your bags, be with your mother."

You first.

Her fingers curled round the edges of her chair. "I must not be explaining this correctly—"

"I guarantee the world will continue turning in your absence," he interrupted gently, circling round the desk and lifting her to her feet. "I guarantee London will be waiting when you get back."

"Yes, but—"

"Go."

Chapter 2

Molly drove home in a glassy-eyed daze, completely unsurprised when the sunshine vanished and it started to rain. The miles passed quickly, and she was just pulling onto her street, when her phone beeped with a classic distress cry from her best friend.

I think I'm going to start taking vitamins.

"Bloody hell..."

She spun the wheel away from the curb and kept driving, rolling to a stop in front of the Wardell's house instead. The front door was locked, but she'd made herself a key the day after Devon and Julian had purchased the property almost ten years earlier. A few seconds later, she was bursting through the doorway, circling the empty rooms, before racing to the attic instead.

"There you are!" she exclaimed, finding a pale girl with a halo of dark hair lying on her back in the center of the room. "I got here as fast as I could!"

Rae lifted her head in surprise. "Did you drive?"

"I was coming from Guilder," Molly answered dryly, slinging her purse to the floor and lying down beside her. "You'll never guess what happened to me today..."

It only took a few minutes to recount the dreadful tale. Another few minutes after that, for Rae to stop swearing violently on her behalf and admit she was second-guessing the vitamins. When the dust finally settled, the two girls lay down once more, staring at the ceiling, lost in their thoughts.

"Knee replacement, huh?" Rae murmured. "Like she needed to be move faster."

Molly shuddered, wrapping both arms around her waist. "It's going to be a nightmare. And you know what? My dad knows it! What was he thinking—going lambing at a time like this?!"

There was a creak of floorboards as Rae tilted her head in surprise.

"Wait...*lambing*?" she repeated incredulously. "As in...baby sheep? I thought you said he was going to be off laughing with your Uncle Charlie."

"*Lambing*," Molly repeated, over-enunciating the word. "Every spring, the farmers help to deliver a thousand little babies in the middle of a field. It's like Woodstock, but for sheep."

"Yeah, that makes more sense," Rae murmured, turning back to the ceiling with a frown. "Your dad's always fancied himself a farmer. And as I remember, Uncle Charlie doesn't laugh a lot."

Molly shot her a guilty look. "I tried to send Luke in my place."

"Ha!" Rae let out a burst of laughter, swatting her at the same time. "You're lucky he made it back the first time! Didn't the guy try to shave his head?"

"He actually did a little. But it was in the back." Molly opened her mouth to say something further, then closed it with a sigh. "It's just going to be the same three conversations that we always have. Why can't I look a little different? Why can't I act a little different? And why couldn't I have married a different guy?" She caught Rae's questioning gaze. "She would have preferred Julian."

"Ah, I see." Rae leaned back, folding her hands behind her head. "If it's any consolation, I'm sure my dad would have preferred that I'd married Julian as well. Or Gabriel. Yeah, probably Gabriel."

Molly rolled her eyes at the ceiling. "You think that makes me feel better? Having you compare your psychopathic father to my mom?" They shared a look, then shrugged and resettled. "Yeah, that's not really a stretch." She bit restlessly at her lip before letting out a frustrated sigh.

"You know the thing that gets me? It's not even that he's leaving me with her. She's my mom and she needs help—of course I'll be there for that. It's that he's trying to pretend like there's nothing strange about it. Like everything's going to be totally fine."

Rae nodded, knowing better than to try and speak.

Molly propped onto her elbows, seized with a sudden thought. "Is he even going with my uncle? Are there even any sheep? For all I know, he's going to be hiding in the attic with recording equipment, performing some kind of psychological experiment—"

There was a scuffling noise just above.

Both girls stopped talking at once, staring at a fixed point on the ceiling. For a few seconds, they simply waited to see what might happen next. Then Rae cupped both hands over her mouth.

"Holy crap," she whispered. "That's definitely a rat."

Typical.

"Maybe it's a shifter," Molly answered hopefully.

Rae shot her a sideways look. "Would that honestly be any better? Think about what you just said."

They considered in silence, then turned back to the ceiling—unable to decide.

Another faint scuffling, followed by a distinct scratching sound that felt very much like a threat. At that point, both of the girls lifted to their feet, backing slowly toward the wall.

Rae swallowed hard, lifting her hands into the air.

"Do you think I should use lava, or—"

A door opened beneath them, and the creature darted away.

Oh, thank goodness.

"Honey?"

Devon's voice filtered up the stairs.

"Just a second!" Rae called back, dusting off her clothes. "I made a pitcher of strawberry margaritas. Want to help me finish it off? We can toast your last night in civilization."

"Absolutely."

Molly recovered her purse and headed toward the stairs before pausing suddenly in the doorway. "I almost forgot, did you break Devon and forget to tell me? Like last night? ...in bed?"

"Oh—that." Rae's eyes twinkled with mischief. "We were trying something new..."

That's my girl.

DEVON WAS ALREADY RUMMAGING around in the refrigerator by the time the girls got down to the kitchen—having successfully re-parked Molly's car so it wasn't on his front lawn. He'd refused to confess his injury to Alicia, then got thoroughly trounced by a forty-year-old shifter on the sparring mats—a man who'd zeroed in on those precise muscles with uncanny focus. Fortunately, there had only been a few agents left training, and he'd already vowed never to tell his wife.

"How's the arm?" Molly asked innocently, sweeping inside.

He froze mid-step, looking as though he might be sick. Rae walked in just a second behind her, giving him a kiss on the cheek, followed by an oblivious squeeze.

"A few hours ago, Gabriel just texted me a string of smiley faces." She glanced again at her phone before slipping it into her pocket. "You wouldn't know anything about that, would you?"

He took a deep breath, then decided to simply start over. "Strawberry margaritas, huh? You ladies having some fun?"

Molly reached for some glasses, while Rae shot him a significant look.

"Molly got a call about her mom."

His face went suddenly pale. "Oh"—he shut the refrigerator quickly—"well, I'll just—"

"Have a drink with us."

His eyes strayed to the fruity pink cocktail before drifting back to the women. With the words 'Molly's mom' still ringing in his ears, he backed to the door with a trace of panic.

"That's sweet, but I'm sure you girls want some—"

"Have a bloody drink."

Less than a minute later, the three of them were sitting at the table. Unable to locate the correct glasses, Rae had conjured the biggest tumblers she was able and stuffed them with tiny umbrellas. She then summoned a trio of sunhats to complete the mood, despite the English rain.

"How do you even...?" Devon picked his drink up hesitantly, batting away the toys and searching for the best way to approach. "Do you need some kind of straw?"

His wife kicked him beneath the table.

"So when would you leave?" she asked seriously.

When *would* you leave, not when *do* you leave. They were still rooted firmly in the subjunctive, and Molly very much appreciated the distinction.

"Well, my dad already left, so I'd probably head out tomorrow morning. His part of the lambing only lasts a few days, then he can come back and take over."

"Is she already up and walking around?"

"I'm sure she walked right out of the hospital. I'm sure she's using her crutches like a spear."

Devon stared incredulously between them, half-shaded by the brim of his floppy hat. "I'm sorry," he inserted cautiously, hesitant to call attention to himself, "what exactly is going on with your mom? And did you just say *lambing*?"

An errant thought froze him in his chair. "Molls, what is your mother doing with the lambs—"

Rae kicked him again, but Molly snorted with laughter.

"You mean, is she performing some kind of ritual sacrifice to remove my ink and make me her favorite shade of brunette? No, thank goodness. Not this time. She had a knee replacement. My dad wants me to come out there for a few days and help take care of her."

He leaned back in surprise, playing absentmindedly with an umbrella.

"Oh—shite. I'm sorry." He paused again, already feeling the buzz of his wife's heavy-handed tequila. "Is that why you were at the Oratory today? Were you requesting a leave of absence?"

I was requesting the equivalent of a doctor's note.

"It's complicated to explain," Molly answered delicately, stabbing into the pink sludge with the spear of her umbrella. "Mostly I was just helping him with a bison problem."

Rae nodded knowingly. "Was Craig at it with the faucets again?"

The three friends let out a martyred sigh, then returned to their drinks.

This is why I can't leave—right there.

Over the years, the makeshift family had waded through a hundred such conversations and developed an impeccable balance for the line between the supernatural and the mundane. She could not return to a place where one was completely ignored, leaving her to drown in the other.

Devon lifted his eyes cautiously, feeling dangerously emboldened by his margarita. "So I take it you and your mom haven't talked again about the tatù—"

Rae smacked him furiously, then turned to Molly with misty eyes.

"But you guys haven't talked again about the tatù?"

He stared between them in complete bewilderment, while Molly let out another sigh. The tequila was working on her, too. Settling in with a grim kind of resignation.

"Not everyone could be as cool about it as your mom, Dev."

It was a rather large over-simplification, but the essence remained true. His mother had accepted what he'd told her just because he was the one to say it. She'd examined the ink on his arm, kissed him on the cheek, then the two of them had proceeded to sit down and eat pie.

Of course, she'd spent the next seven months digging frantically through the internet for anything to help her make sense of what was happening. She'd rubberized the countertops in the kitchen on the off-chance he managed to hurt himself. She's started a diary and stopped eating pie.

It's a lot better than my mom.

He flashed a sympathetic smile.

"It didn't go that well for Rae, either." He cast a sideways glance at his wife. "Remember when your Uncle Argyle told your Aunt Linda? She fainted while she was holding the family cat."

Rae shuddered at the memory. One precautionary vet visit and a bottle of valium later, her aunt had yet to fully recover. Her uncle still carried the scars from it upon his arm.

"I always forget about that cat," Molly murmured. "How is that thing possibly still alive?"

"I keep healing him," Rae whispered conspiratorially.

Devon stifled a grin, squeezing her hand beneath the table.

He carefully removed the sunhat and placed it on the table in front of him. The drink, he kept. In spite of his visceral aversion to the color, he had grown impossibly attached.

"Honey, you know it's going to be fine. One way or another, it's just a few days and then you're back. You're a spy, Molls. You can do anything for a few days. Jules and I once pretended we spoke Russian for a week in a St. Petersburg's prison. No one was the wiser."

Molly nodded glumly, then stopped herself all at once.

"Didn't they have you committed—"

"Ignore him," Rae instructed, throwing her husband a derisive look. "I shouldn't have given him so many umbrellas. But you know that he's right," she added in a quieter voice. "It's only for a little while, and if things start to implode, just call me and I'll be on the next plane."

The sunhat wilted and Molly let out a little sigh.

"You promise?"

"Cross my heart."

BY THE TIME MOLLY FINALLY made it home that evening, Benji had already been tucked in for the night and Luke was waiting for her in the foyer, holding a box of Welsh candy.

"What's that?" she asked, setting her purse on the counter.

"A bribe," he answered with a grin, lifting it tauntingly out of reach. "From your dad, I think. It came this afternoon."

"Don't eat that, it's mine." She jumped up to grab it, then stuffed one into her mouth, shaking the box suspiciously. "This is half-empty."

"You were gone a long time."

She snorted with laughter, shaking it again. "It came this afternoon? He only called this morning."

Luke shrugged, pacing into the kitchen to finish cleaning the dishes. "The man has talent. I can see where you get it."

She trailed listlessly after him, feeling her window of escape closing with every step. Unable to put that to words, she hopped onto the counter instead, determined to change the subject.

"I still can't believe you hacked Benji's robot."

"You can hack into anything," he answered absentmindedly. "I hacked into our coffeemaker. Made it do all sorts of frightful things."

She forced herself to smile, staring down at her hands.

"He's going to be so disappointed. He and Aria have been grooming that thing for weeks. If their creepy drawings are any indication, they were planning on using it to take over the world."

Luke chuckled without glancing up from the sink. "So many times we've stopped that from happening," he murmured. "It would be a real shame if our kids were the ones who finally did it."

When there wasn't a reply, he glanced over his shoulder—only to find his lovely wife staring in deflated silence at the countertop, those precious chocolates melting unnoticed in her hands.

He abandoned the dishes immediately, pressing a kiss to her temple. "Hey, come here..."

They flipped off the lights and headed down the hall, curling onto the giant bed she'd returned three times before deciding it could be allowed to stay. The blankets were whisper-soft beneath them, a shimmering gray with just the faintest traces of blue.

"Talk to me." Luke slipped off her sweater, pressing another kiss to her neck. "What's going on inside that head of yours?"

She shivered a little, leaning back into his arms. "He won't be there," she whispered, finally putting it to words. "He's always been there, standing between us. We've *needed* something between us. Now it's just going to be me?"

Luke tightened his grip, resting his chin upon her shoulder. "Do you want me to come? I could bring Benji. We could make it a family trip."

It was tempting. *So very* tempting. When she twisted around and looked at him, she was tempted all the more. But then a flash of something like defiance spiked suddenly in her blood.

"That's sweet." She kissed him. "Very sweet. But there's no need for the Highlands to claim all of us. You stay here and watch the kid. I'll handle my mother."

Even as she said the words, she shuddered again.

No one *handled* her mother.

"For what it's worth"—Luke twisted her around, pulling him into her lap—"I've met your mother. Several times." His eyes twinkled and he whispered into her ear. "My money's on you."

She looked at him hopefully. "Really?"

He nodded silently, tracing a finger across her lower lip. "So if you're leaving tomorrow morning, let's make the most of tonight."

He tipped her suddenly backward and when she giggled and tried to sit up, he knocked her back down with the tips of his fingers, sinking down in front of her, grinning wickedly all the while.

"You've had a rough day," he said innocently, kissing her knee, "why don't you lay back and let me handle things for a while…"

She sucked in a quick breath, letting her head fall back on the pillows.

The tequila had her spinning, her husband was only trying to making things seem better, and there, in the comfort of her oversized English bed, it was easier to put things into perspective.

"You're right, it's going to be fine," she breathed. "It's only for a few days. I could speak Russian, and ration these chocolates, and keep myself from killing her that long."

He cast her a quick look, then continued in earnest.

It could be worse, I would be lambing on the moors…

Chapter 3

I *would give ANYTHING to be lambing on the moors.*

Less than twenty-four hours after receiving the call from her father, Molly was standing on the ground floor of Inverness Airport, staring dolefully out the window at the heavy Scottish rain.

There had been mechanical trouble on the first plane she'd been seated on. Inclement weather had grounded the second. By the time she secured herself a ticket on the third, the craft they wheeled out looked like a slightly larger version of some of the build-it-yourself kits that Benji played with back home. She'd stepped aboard carefully, eyeing the rickety stairs and wondering if the screws could possibly keep it together, then she held her breath for the whole eighty-minute flight.

She'd touched down a few minutes ago...only to discover the latest mishap.

"Are you Ms. Skye?"

She whirled around with a start, lifting her eyes to take in the full scale of the man standing behind her, whilst trying to decipher anything past the thick Scottish brogue. He was a giant, as were so many of his kinsmen. And judging by the red-inked clipboard, he didn't come bearing good news.

"Yes, that's me. I'm Molly." She fidgeted nervously, wringing her hands and bracing for the worst. "Were you able to find my bags?"

His eyes twinkled, bright blue against the gray fraying of his beard. "Your *eight* bags?" he asked innocently. "That's a lot of clothes for a wee little thing like yourself. Yes, I was able to find them. But I'm sorry to say, they didn't make the flight."

She let out a slow breath, stomach dropping to the floor.

Of course they didn't.

"...do you know why?"

"The report wasn't specific," he answered dutifully, "so I'm not entirely sure. It might have been a size component, or perhaps they simply exceeded the weight limit for the plane."

It was hard to say for sure, but he might have been enjoying himself.

"Well, maybe if the plane wasn't the size of a toy—" She caught herself quickly, making a mental tally of everything that was lost. "Do you have any idea where they ended up?"

"*That* I do know!" He scanned quickly down the clipboard before jamming his finger into a particular spot. "It seems those bags never got off the first plane you were scheduled to fly on this morning. A Boeing 747 that was rerouted to...Phnom Penh."

There was a pause.

"That's the capital of Cambodia."

She dug her fingernails into her palms, trying hard to control the waves of electric current that were racing beneath her skin. "I know where it is, thank you."

I arrested a gun-runner there last month.

"If you'd like to provide us with a forwarding address, we can have them sent to your residence in Scotland. I can even guarantee expedience. No longer than six or seven weeks."

Their eyes met slowly. His twinkled like a cartoon.

Yes, he's definitely enjoying himself.

She pulled in a deep breath, then let it out at a measured speed—pushing back all those clamoring 'first' emotions and reaching for the steadier ones in back.

Whatever this teasing, grandfatherly man might be seeing in front of him, it was a nothing more than a common world illusion. The hydraulic machinery, the teams of security, the raging weather...the most dangerous thing in the airport was the petite redhead clutching her purse.

You cannot blow up the airport. This isn't a mission. You're not Angel. Besides, that's just a stalling tactic to avoid going to the house.

"Forget the bags," she said calmly, "I won't be here that long. Can you just point me toward the taxis? Or has the country finally discovered Uber? I'm only going to Evanton."

"Aw, you're going to Evanton?" he repeated in delight, lowering the clipboard as if they'd love nothing more than to swap tales. "Tell me, love, have you got family there? I would have mourned your bags better, if you'd told me—"

"Is there a taxi service?" she repeated, balling her fingers into crackling fists.

He studied her a moment, eyes dancing. Then he pointed down the road. "Of course there is. What do you take us for—a colony?" He chuckled under his breath. "Of course, it's more of a single taxi, than a whole service. But I can tell you the driver's name is Ellis, he'll run you a fair price...and he's been out sick since last Thursday. There are no taxis."

She took a reflexive step down the pavement, then caught herself just as fast. "Wait, there are no—"

"No taxis, no buses. No...*Uber*. Not at this time of day, and not in that direction. That being said, it's only fifteen miles or so up the road. I'm sure someone is headed to the same place."

Her body froze a moment in sheer astonishment before she threw open her arms. "*That's* your advice?!" she cried. "After you lost my luggage, after you passive-aggressively criticized my packing?" Her finger jabbed into the air. "Yes, you did. Don't look at me like that, you did. *That's* the advice you're going to offer a young woman travelling by herself? To hitchhike?"

Her chest heaved from the rant, from the cold, and from the thick scent of heather, but she kept her finger leveled between them. The man might have been a relic from another time, but she'd travelled the world and battled giants of her own—giants a lot scarier than this.

He gazed at her for a moment, then leaned down with an affectionate smile.

"Well, it's not like you'll have to carry any bags."

"COME ON...PICK UP."

Molly tapped nervously on the side of her phone, eyeing the churning storm clouds above.

A few years earlier, Rae had gotten her hands on a teleportation tatù from a man they were interrogating in Brooklyn. But despite the increasingly self-serving protests from her friends, she had yet to master it. Sure, she could conjure new luggage—the same way that she'd conjured the eight bags that had gone missing—but she'd have to be on Scottish soil to make it happen.

No matter, I have someone else for that.

If he ever picks up the—

"Hello?"

She slumped back into the terminal with an actual sigh of relief. "Hey, Mason! How's your training going?"

After unintentionally banishing his geometry teacher to the airport, Mason Ross had been named the PC's most promising new agent in almost a decade—this from a group of dangerously talented people who were all vying for the title themselves. Devon had been in charge of his actual recruitment, but the gang of friends had all pitched in for his training—rotating through his sparring sessions, and smugly taking credit for any and all progress. He'd become a sort of little brother, the kind who navigated his chaotic new friends with a sense of humor and a purse-lipped smile.

"—over in the field marshal's house," he was saying, "so obviously we couldn't stop there. I tried to take them back across the forest, but the lines—"

"Yeah, that's great," she interrupted, casting a quick glance into the terminal. "So listen, I know those portals of yours can transmit energy, but how do they work in terms of actual people?"

A pair of wide-eyed tourists stopped short, and she covered the phone with a smile.

"Science fair. We've got our fingers crossed." She waited until they were gone, listening to the watery clack of the woman's heels before cupping a hand over the receiver. "Sorry about that. What were you saying about the portals?"

There was a crackling pause.

"They, uh...they don't really work on people. I mean, I've never actually tried it before," he clarified. "I've been working with some astrophysicists Carter brought in from Geneva, and they always say it's not meant for people. Something about the rearrangement of subatomic particles."

Molly considered for a moment.

She's come through worse.

"That's okay, there's a first time for everything." She squinted at the rain and backed further under the awning. "I want you to hang up and then call Rae, alright? I'll text you the number."

"I have the number, Molly. But why do you want me to—"

"Doesn't matter," she interrupted calmly, "just get her down to the Oratory, and have her call me back immediately. There's a bit of a time issue, so you'll need to..."

There was a scuffle, then a new voice rang across the line.

"You're in a Scottish airport, Molls. Why exactly are you summoning my wife to Guilder?"

Shit.

"Devon?" Molly flashed a quick look in either direction before peering suspiciously up at the security cameras. "Are you training with Mason?"

"Sure am, sweetheart."

...well that's just terrible luck.

She bit her lower lip, hedging her bets. "Okay, did you happen to be standing close enough to—"

"Now *what's* this I hear about astrophysical experimentation?" he interrupted cheerfully. "And *what* might it have to do with the love of my life?"

She pulled in a deep breath, then decided to level with him. "Dev, they lost my luggage. I'm stranded with no clothes."

There was a pause.

"And you decided to use my wife as a subatomic guinea pig?"

Probably best not to answer that one.

"No clothes, Devon," she repeated, speaking directly into the receiver. "Is there static? I am in Scotland. I am standing in the rain. And I have no clothes. Teleportation is our only option."

There was another pause, a much longer one. Molly cast a look at the phone, hoping things were already underway. Devon cast a look at the ceiling, summoning the very last of his patience.

"Is there a gift shop?"

She pulled back in surprise, thinking she must have misheard. "You're asking about a gift shop?" she repeated incredulously. "You seriously think I'm in the mood to get you presents, when you're standing between me and my missing clothes?"

A faint chorus of laughter echoed in the background, followed by a loud smack.

"Molly,"—Devon gripped the phone hard, oblivious to the little cracks that started spider-webbing beneath his fingers—"a gift shop sells clothes. Don't you think that instead of turning my wife into some kind of gelatinous monster, it might be a better idea to just walk back inside?"

She frowned suspiciously, unable to tell if he was joking. "You really don't *get* clothes, do you?"

The line went dead.

Dev?

"Shit."

A flash of lightning split the sky.

"Shit."

She ducked inside with a gasp, flinging raindrops from her hair and lifting her eyes to the heavens with a watery scowl. Since the day she'd turned sixteen, she'd hated thunderstorms. It felt highly disconcerting whenever those celestial bolts came from something other than herself.

Alright...gift shop.

She cringed at the mere idea, scanning around the terminal.

Another plane had just landed, and the main lobby was packed from wall to wall, crammed to the brink with happy, boisterous people, clutching steaming drinks and chattering all the while. But she still managed to catch sight of a blinking neon storefront. It was actually rather hard to miss.

Oh look, she thought glumly, *there amidst all the fluorescence...clothes.*

With the look of a girl approaching the gallows, she trudged straight through the center of the crowd and ducked into the shop, deciding to ease her way gradually toward the polyester by starting near the magazines instead. She grabbed a few at random—most of them sporting corsets, the others sporting brides—then took the plunge and headed straight for the shelves of athleisure-ware in the back. They were sized to fit the local population and dyed a vibrant array of colors usually reserved for children's ice cream. She took one between her fingers, grimacing all the while.

Oh, sweetheart, what happened to you...?

A bug-eyed woman popped out of nowhere, flashing a Vaseline smile.

"Hello there. Can I help you find anything? I saw you walk in—everyone did. You're hard to miss with that lovely hair. Did you want to get one of the sweatshirts? They're two for twenty."

Molly blinked slowly, then looked down at the monstrosity in her hand. "I'm sorry...two for twenty?"

Is that retail code?

"Two hoodies for just twenty pounds," the woman clarified, lifting a noxious purple sample off the shelf. "These ones are actually quite popular because you can remove the hood by unzipping it here, and with the wicking along the seams, they're reversible."

It flipped inside out with an artificial *pop.*

"Pretty handy, right?"

Molly swallowed hard, then backed away.

"Pretty handy," she echoed, feeling suddenly faint. A flash of lightning electrified the woman's fixed smile, and she clutched the magazines to her chest. "I'll probably just stick to these."

They were scanned and bagged a moment later.

"Are you sure?" the woman asked, printing out the receipt. "The weather's just getting worse and that's a thin sweater you're wearing. Might want to bundle up a little, keep yourself dry."

"What—*that*?" Molly laughed lightly, waving a dismissive hand at the sky. "That'll be gone before we know it. Trust me, storms like this can't sustain those winds for very—"

The terminal shook with thunder and the lights flickered in the shop. A shockwave rippled through the people hurrying outside, making each of them pause and look skyward, before laughing it off. What did they care about the rain? This was Scotland. They had dressed for the weather.

The two women stared at each other, then Molly took the purple hoodie.

"...just in case."

Chapter 4

The weather showed no signs of abating, but the little airport was quickly emptying out, full of people who'd actually made travel arrangements to get themselves further inside the city. Left with few other options, Molly milled about the thinning crowd, wondering if she'd be reprimanded for requesting an extraction team, before venturing outside to the curb herself.

"Excuse me." She caught the sleeve of a passing security guard. "You wouldn't happen to know if there was a taxi or shuttle service to Evanton, would you? I think the guy I asked before might have been messing with me—"

"There's nothing like that around here, love," he answered briskly, heaving a trio of traffic cones along the slick pavement. "We usually have a taxi that covers the rural areas, but Ellis is out sick, and the men who operate the shuttle service are all out lambing on the—"

She held up a hand, biting the inside of her cheek.

"There has to be something," she insisted. "Surely you people can't just abandon travelers the second they land on Scottish soil. People are flying into an airport! It's not like they're arriving with cars! What provisions have been made for the rest of us?!"

Her voice had picked up speed by the end, courtesy of the nine hours it had taken to complete an hour long trip. The wind picked up around her, shivering right through her silken blouse, and in a second of pure madness, she almost found herself reaching for the sweatshirt.

The man regarded her for a moment, then tilted his head with a smile.

"The rest of us?" he repeated sharply. "The rest of us usually make arrangements ahead of time, so we don't find ourselves in this situation. The rest of us usually stay in the city and don't antagonize the residents. But if you'd like to file a complaint, I'd be happy to take it down myself."

She stared back at him in silence, not entirely convinced that was true.

"You're heading to Evanton?"

A raspy voice cut above the wind, and both Molly and the security guard turned to see grizzled old man in a down jacket and suspenders. He was standing in front of an open-bed truck that had been so overloaded with straw, little bits of it were blowing off into the storm. For the life of her, she didn't understand why he'd found himself at the airport. He would have been more at home in the dustbowl or Appalachia. Or perhaps tending to his flock in the fields of Middle Earth.

"Ah—see?" The security guard clapped her on the shoulders, before pacing away with a grin he did nothing to hide. "That's hospitality for you."

She ignored him, taking a tentative step forward. "You're going to Evanton?"

"Just passing through, but you're welcome to hitch a ride." He cocked a finger toward the truck. "Not much room in the front, but the back's wide open and we're not going far."

Her eyes flitted to the bales of hay.

...in there?

She smiled gratefully, but couldn't bring herself to move—struck with a sudden flashback of being faced with a similar situation in the sixteen hundreds, when her friends were being chased by a gang of thugs and smuggled themselves into the city inside a wagon loaded down with rotting fruit.

Valium got you through that. Valium can get you through this as well.

"That's...that's very generous of you." She approached cautiously, shaking his hand with a water-logged smile. "Thank you very much."

His eyes twinkled as they swept her up and down. "You're sure travelling light. Didn't bring any bags?"

She hesitated a split second, then heaved herself into the straw. "No...no bags."

IT WAS ONLY A TWENTY-minute drive from the airport to the tiny village of Evanton, but it felt a great deal longer than that, bouncing along in the back of a feed truck. Oddly enough, Molly didn't really mind. The rain had stopped almost immediately when they set out from the city, and despite her instinctual draw toward the finer things, she'd spent the last few years roughing it out in situations a hell of a lot worse. Instead of attempting to balance herself and perch upon the wooden railing, she nestled further into the straw—staring out with an unexpected feeling of nostalgia over the rolling greens and flower-speckled violets of her adopted home.

She hadn't grown up in Scotland, though they often visited family. She'd grown up in a city in Wales. A lovely city, the kind people didn't often leave, which was why she was flat-out stunned when her mother announced one day they'd sold the house and were headed for the Highlands.

At the time, she'd made it her personal mission to uncover the reason.

Rae's mother lived in Scotland and there had always been a strange competition between the two women, a competition that only one of them was actually aware of. Her father wanted to 'get back to nature,' and her mother despised the neighbor's dog, so that might have been it. But try as she might to bolster herself up with excuses, the timing of the move gave the reason away.

It happened to coincide directly with her sixteenth birthday.

She let out a quiet sigh, drawing her knees up to her chest. Best not to think about anything like that now. It wasn't like they'd ever spoken about it openly. Passive-aggressive deflection and fierce compartmen-talization—that was the Skye family recipe, perfected over the genera-tions.

Probably why I got myself a new family.

With a sudden ache of longing, she fished her phone from the pocket of her new hoodie and pressed a number on speed dial, waiting through the rings until her husband picked up.

"Hey, Molls!"

She lowered her voice dramatically, speaking directly into the re-ceiver. "Will you accept a collect call from HMP Brixton Correctional Facility?"

Luke extracted himself from a meeting with a beaming smile, jog-ging casually up the ancient steps of the Abbey before swinging himself one-handed onto the roof. One of the problems with life in the old monastery, was a lack of cell reception. One of the many, *many* prob-lems.

"I was expecting to hear from you hours ago. How's the trip go-ing?"

Funny you should ask...

She took a quick picture and sent it his way. "Hang on."

There was a long pause, then his voice crackled tentatively through the line.

"...are you in a feed truck?"

"Yep—I am currently riding in a feed truck. Without any luggage. To a small village in the middle of the Scotland. Nothing but me and my mother...and her bionic knee."

There was another pause.

"...are you in a hoodie?"

"How are things back in London?" she diverted quickly, tightening the purple drawstrings until she started to choke. "Did the foundations start to crumble the second I left?"

He chuckled quietly, gazing down at the people below. "I'm actually at the Abbey. My dad called an emergency meeting to discuss all the discord happening between Carter and Barnes. They're trying to find a way to stay neutral."

Good luck with that.

Over the last few months, the 'Barnes Dilemma' had grown in size and velocity, until what had started as a little turbulence had swelled into a raging storm. The things he was proposing were ridiculous—absolutely ridiculous. To expose their tatùs to the common world, to introduce the idea of people with powers...it went against everything the supernatural community was built upon.

But some could say that Carter planted the idea himself, when he opened the doors to the school. Still others could argue that 'common world transparency' was the natural progression in a secret that was always too vast and fantastical to keep. The friends had picked a clear side, along with many others. But another side was growing as well—as volatile as it was restless.

Yet another reason I should have stayed in London.

"Wait, you're taking a call at the Abbey?" she asked suddenly, now openly chewing on the drawstring. "Are you standing on the roof? Are you holding up your hand like an antenna?"

"No, why would you—" He quickly lowered his hand. "I am not holding up my hand like a bloody antenna. This is a state-of-the-art facility, you snob. I can take a phone call."

"Don't be proud, Luke. If anyone asks, just say you're doing yoga."

He stifled a grin, raising his arm once again. "I'm proud of you for going," he said quietly. "Did I mention that?"

She drew in a silent breath, then poked a finger petulantly into the straw. "I'm...trying to see the positives. It's beautiful here," she admitted, gazing out over the endless fields. "I'd forgotten how beautiful. We should take Benji more often."

Her son had been quite taken with the Highlands the last time they'd visited. He'd promptly fashioned himself a crown made of heather and declared himself king.

"This is one of those things, Molly," Luke murmured, remembering the same image with a tender smile. "This is one of those things that feels impossible now, but your mom's going to look back on this and be grateful you were there. Who knows? Maybe it could be the start of something."

He knew better than to add that last part. She knew better than to believe it. But there in the wide, open fields of Scotland, drinking in breaths of the misty green air, it felt like the kind of place where things like that *were* possible. Where sunlight was magic and the rules didn't apply.

Molly smiled in spite of herself, pressing the phone to her cheek. "Rescue me in five days?"

He chuckled under his breath. "I'd rescue you in four."

THE SUN WAS JUST SLIPPING below the hills when the little feed cart rolled down the bumpy road into Evanton. They'd stopped twice so the driver could call back with some urgent comment on the scenery. They'd stopped a third time so that Molly could climb down and be sick. By the time they pulled onto the familiar streets, she was feeling decidedly worse for wear, yet oddly determined.

Luke is right...this is going to be good for us.

She hopped down from the truck, shaking little bits of straw and stray dandelion seeds from her hair. The sweatshirt was damp, but not unwearable. The make-up had miraculously survived.

"Thank you so much!" she called, waving to the driver with a bright smile. "I still have no earthly idea what you mean by 'mulching,' but I think your garden's off to a great start!"

He chuckled loudly and pulled away down road—whistling the same tune he'd been singing that morning. The same tune he'd been singing the morning before that.

She stared after him, squinting into the setting sun.

This is going to be a part of the story we tell each other. Years from now, when everything's fine.

Still clutching that same hopeful breath in her chest, she rotated slowly and fixed her eyes on the house at the end of the flowering lane. It was perfect, but of course it was. Her mother had designed every inch of it. And her mother never tolerated anything less than perfection.

With a pair of nervous, fluttery hands, she smoothed herself all over and wished she'd been able to glimpse her reflection in the mirror of the truck. The tiny one in her compact had appeared deceptively composed, but then again, she'd only caught a quick glance at her face.

Stop worrying about your reflection. That doesn't matter.

Go knock on the door.

With another deep breath, she strode abruptly forward and lifted the brass knocker, tapping three times with a deceptively resonate *boom*. She waited as collectedly as she could, picturing her mother glancing up in surprise, imagining her hobbling down the stairs, worrying that her leg had kept her bedridden and she couldn't hobble, panicked she didn't know her daughter was coming.

A century crawled past, when really it was only a few seconds. By now, the image had firmly ingrained of her mother waiting behind the door with a knife. Molly had just resolved to sleep in a ditch and come back in the morning, when the door swept suddenly open, blowing back her hair.

"Molly Elizabeth Skye." The voice raked into her, like nails through butter. "Things might be different in England, but have you been sleeping in a barn?"

Chapter 5

"*He didn't tell her I was coming!*"

Molly was crouched in the shower, fully clothed, cupping one hand over the receiver of her phone, while the other knotted manically in her hair. She'd gotten up at the crack of dawn, a truly spectacular feat for those who knew her, just to make the call in private. Things like privacy were in short supply in such a place. So were unmonitored phone calls. Like prison.

"Hold on." Rae stepped away from a sparring session, unwrapping the tape from her knuckles as a long dark ponytail cascaded down her back. "You're saying that your dad—"

"—didn't tell my mother that I was coming," Molly hissed, casting furtive glances at the door. "He took care of all the logistics for the next few days, let her think that she'd be alone until he got back, then lo and behold—her unwanted *daughter* shows up at the front door!"

A burst of sparks fell harmlessly onto the tile.

It was why she tended to make those kinds of calls in the tub.

"So I take it things are going well?" Rae asked sweetly. "At any rate, she hasn't confiscated your phone yet. Devon was super pissed at you, by the way. Did you try to have me melted?"

"One day at a time, Kerrigan," Molly growled. "That was *yesterday*. Let's focus on *today*. How am I supposed to do this? She didn't even *talk* to me last night. She took a single look, said that I'd missed dinner, and that I should probably take some of the straw out of my hair before going to bed. *Some* of the straw. She seemed to assume there would always be some percentage that stayed."

There was a pause.

"Why was there—"

"Focus!"

"Right—sorry." Rae chewed her lip helplessly, firing off a distracted cyclone to keep her sparring partners at bay. "Well, usually I'd say this was a bad reaction to the pain medication, but if we're being honest, that's pretty much just Eleanor. How's her knee?"

"I bet the whole thing is metal now," Molly whispered, crouching lower in the tub. "Rae, it's only made her stronger. I'm starting to think she got one on purpose."

Her friend nodded grimly. "Well, you know what they say about metal."

Molly flashed another glare at the door, fingers crackling. "It's highly conductive?"

"What—no. Molly, put your hands down."

How does she know about my hands?

"Remember that terrible lady who ran the ramen place by the cemetery? She didn't have a heart, so the good people at St. Thomas' Hospital gave her one?"

Molly frowned at the phone. "Are you talking about Mrs. Wu's cardio-transplant?"

"It saved her life, Molly. But more than that, it saved her reputation. It gave her a reason to keep getting up in the morning, to pick up her broom, and keep chasing all those kids."

She started taking the vitamins.

"This is veering off a little," Molly answered warily. "What are you trying to—"

"Your mom could be the same way. All she needed was a few extra parts."

At that point, Molly was caught directly between a laugh and a scream. Seeing as both of them would wake her mother, she threw a lightning bolt out the window and cursed instead.

"Let me get this straight: you think the metal is *humanizing* her?" She closed her eyes, not knowing where to start. "Rae, there's like...a whole genre of movies you need to watch."

Terminator. Blade Runner.

Apollo 13.

"Just hear me out—"

"No, this has already reached critical levels and we haven't even sat down for breakfast. I am hiding in a *shower* right now, and I'm telling you, we have passed the point of no return."

There was a moment of silence.

"What do you need?"

Finally, she asks.

"Okay, it's going to sound a little crazy, but bear with me: I'm going to need you to break into Carter's office and forge his authorization for emergency use of the jet." Molly raised a hand, braced for the subsequent protest. "And yes, I know he told us not to 'borrow' it again, but Rae, this time will be different. Once you're up in the air, we're only going to have a brief window before—"

The shower curtain ripped open.

"...I have to go."

The line went dead and Molly lifted her eyes slowly—staring into an eerie self-portrait, aged about thirty years' time. The hair was copper-red, but had been allowed to wane gracefully with swirls of silver. The skin had been preserved to perfection, bolstered with every pharmaceutical wonder-cream known to man. The mouth had been painted to appear deceptively soft, while a circle of pearls clung tight to the neck. All the ingredients were the same, and in a cosmic attempt at humor, the resemblance between the two was uncanny. The only thing different was the eyes. Her mother had grey eyes—a ring of bright iron, like the chilled waters of an unchanging sea.

"Are you going to sit in the tub all day? Or do you think you might come downstairs for a civilized breakfast? I don't know how it goes in England, but we still do that at this time of the day."

And so it begins...

Molly pushed slowly to her feet, sliding the phone discreetly into her sleeve.

"Breakfast sounds lovely," she said through a fixed smile. "And yes, that's a custom we have in England. Although we often exchange tea for proper caffeine."

"Barbaric."

Eleanor picked an imaginary speck of lint from her sleeve, another delicate strand of pearls jangling from her wrist. They were oddly chain-like. As if one wasn't allowing the other to leave.

"Did you get the chocolates your father sent?"

Molly nodded swiftly, feeling ridiculous to still be standing in the tub. "I have so many memories of those. It was like eating a piece of my childhood."

Silence.

"Why must you make everything sound so vulgar?"

More silence.

"How is that *vulgar*?"

Their eyes met for a moment, then flashed opposite directions.

"Come downstairs." Her mother swept to the door without a backward glance, pausing only to flash a wry smile from the frame. "I made crêpes."

IT WAS STILL A FEW minutes before dawn when Molly jogged downstairs to the kitchen, but her mother was already bustling around the stovetop, pulling down mugs and spoons for tea. She was impeccably dressed, impeccably groomed, and polished to a dangerous shine. If there had been a recent medical trauma, you'd never have known it.

There was nothing but a thin sheen of dew on the tops of her slippers—no doubt from when she'd gone outside to critique the landscapers.

"How was your flight?" she asked without looking, tending to the kettle and setting her crutches to the side. "I would have expected you earlier, if I'd been expecting you at all."

Molly hopped onto the counter, folding up her legs beneath her.

"It was long," she admitted. "I had to change planes once. There was also a storm, and they lost all my luggage." Given the state of her arrival, she felt the need to add, "I had to hitch a ride to town in the back of a feed cart."

Her mother turned around slowly. "Oh dear."

They locked eyes for longer than normal. Molly wasn't breathing, but she could have sworn the woman's lips curved with the hint of a smile. Then she turned back to the stove.

"So what'll it be? Sweet or savory? I've got berries, I've got cream." She glanced around the cabinets. "I could hunt around for some chocolate, but it sounds like you've already eaten your fill. I could make us mimosas—unless you're not drinking." She cast a sudden look over her shoulder. "You're not pregnant, are you?"

Her eyes lingered on the baggy sweatshirt, and Molly balled her hands into fists.

"No, mother. I'm not pregnant."

The refrigerator door swung open.

"We'll have some juice. Just in case."

I should have stayed on the truck.

With a little sigh, Molly hopped down and gathered up the plates and utensils, arranging them on opposite sides of the table, as her mother swept forward with a platter of crêpes. That was the way carbs had always been served in the house. On a platter. As a test. Although she wasn't feeling particularly hungry, Molly took a giant stack and heaped them onto her plate, reaching for the cream.

Her mother returned with a small teacart carrying the tea, watching with a faint smile. "So glad that feed truck didn't diminish your appetite."

Molly cut herself a large piece, answering only when her mouth was full. "I'm steeling myself up. Preparing for battle."

There was actually a bit of laughter at that—gone quickly—as her mother poured the kettle neatly into two cups and sprinkled in a handful of herbs taken directly from the garden. A floral aroma clouded between them, sweetening the air and masking the sharper tang just beneath.

"What is it?" Molly asked curiously, swishing around her cup.

"A blend of rose and Japanese honeysuckle," her mother replied crisply, taking a sip from her own glass. "It's used to ward off unwanted ailments."

She totally looked at ME when she said that.

"So how's life back in England? How's Benji?"

Molly twirled the fork in her fingers, staring down at her plate.

Most people would ask about work. Most people would ask about friends. But she knew that she wasn't going to get any of those questions. Her mother didn't know her friends, with the hard-fought exception of Julian, and she refused to acknowledge things like spies, magic, or the 'tasteless tramp-stamp her daughter had gotten on her sixteenth birthday.' Benji was a safe subject.

Then we'll stick to him.

She took out her phone and pulled up a picture, smiling at it a moment, before tilting the screen toward her mother's eyes. It was a fairly recent one she'd taken of him in the park. Unlike the other children playing quietly the background, he'd removed most of his clothing and was attempting to fashion himself a new wardrobe made of nothing but crumpled leaves and bark.

Eleanor's eyes warmed with a genuine smile. "Look at him," she murmured. "Getting bigger every day."

Molly stared at her across the table before slipping it back into her pocket. "He's a little troublemaker, but his teacher says he's top of the class. The other day he asked Luke to 'borrow the car' so he could drive to the nearest bank and 'borrow some money.'"

She thought it best not to mention the water gun he'd stashed inside his pants.

"That's one way of doing it." Eleanor chuckled again, taking a sip of tea. "You should start hiding your keys, just in case. That's what your father and I always did."

Molly flashed her a quick look, but said nothing.

She'd been highly dubious about the woman's transition into *grandmother*, having experienced her attempts at nurturing firsthand. But she had to admit, she'd been surprised at every turn. When Benji had come to visit, her mother had completely transformed—down on her hands and knees in the garden, roaring like a dinosaur while he squealed with laughter and fended her off with sticks.

I've had dreams like that. They didn't end well.

"So what about you?" she asked abruptly, changing the subject. "How was your *surgery*? You know—the one you forgot to tell me about."

Eleanor flashed a dry smile, then gestured to the counter. "The surgery went fine. The doctors were dull, but competent. They left an entire pharmacy of medication to help ease my transition back into normal life."

Molly's eyes flew to the bottles. "And have you been taking them?"

There was another silence, followed by a sharp smile.

"My threshold for pain is a bit higher than average. I'm saving them for a rainy day."

Of course you are.

Molly pushed up from the table with a scarcely-contained sigh, sweeping across the tile to examine the medication for herself. Sure enough, most of them were unopened. The few that were, had been scribbled upon with instructions in her father's messy hand.

"Mom, you can't just *not* take these," she chided, twisting them around to read. "Most of them aren't even for pain. There are some anti-inflammatories, some muscle relaxers..." She lifted her eyes. "Does Dad know you haven't been taking them? He would be seriously—"

"What your father doesn't know, won't hurt him." Eleanor pushed abruptly to her feet, scraping the chair across the marble. "And why he saw the need to saddle me with a visitor in the middle of my recovery, I will never understand."

...a visitor?

Molly pulled in a sharp breath, fighting to keep her temper.

"He called because he was worried about you, and let me assure you, I'm not going to stay a second longer than I'm needed. But you do *need* some help right now, Mom. Is there a list of doctors I should check in with? Or a physical therapy schedule to—"

"I'm going out."

She stopped short, staring in shock. "You're...what?"

"I'm leaving, darling." Her mother took her purse from the counter, swinging the handle over her crutch with a thin smile. "You should know what that looks like, you've done it often enough. There's some food in the refrigerator, but don't eat anything after six. I'll be coming back and making dinner for the two of us. I can't have you stuffing yourself in the hours before."

It took Molly a second to catch up. By the time she did, her mother was already at the door.

"Hang on!" she called, rushing after her. "You can't just leave, Mom. You need to be resting, and probably not driving. And definitely not walking by yourself."

No answer.

"If you really want to go somewhere, let me come with you. How are you going to drive stick with your left knee?"

Eleanor turned around slowly, pulling a pair of leather gloves over her hands. "I am perfectly capable. I have no desire for a lecture, and I wasn't asking your permission. This is still my house, Molly Elizabeth, and I will go where I please." She paused a moment, letting that sink in, before waving a careless hand around the foyer. "I'll only be a few hours, and there's plenty you can do in the meantime. That dratted agency of yours never sleeps. Perhaps you can catch up on some work."

She was gone a second later, sweeping down the garden lane without a backward glance at her stricken daughter standing on the porch. Molly stared after her in silence, fingers curled into helpless fists by her sides. She stood there until the gate swung shut, then she stormed back into the house and sat down at the kitchen table. She then proceeded to eat her breakfast in silence.

She finished the entire platter of crêpes.

AFTER A SCALDING SHOWER, Molly retreated to her bedroom to regroup.

Breakfast was a disaster, but to be honest, it could have gone much worse. Her clothing situation continued to be a problem, but at the moment, it was of secondary concern.

Where are you...?

She had searched in all the usual places. She had searched with the training and veracity of a spy. And she was still no closer to finding her mother's Wi-Fi password.

In a kind of frenzy, she paced in circles around the living room, feeling like a caged animal, grimacing every time she saw her neon purple reflection sail past in the mirror. After a dozen or so rotations, she finally let out a shriek of frustration and pulled out her phone.

Deep breaths. She can sense distress.

"Hi, Mom."

There was a crackle of static, then a cheerful voice sounded on the line.

"Darling, what an occasion! This is the most you've called me all year."

Molly closed her eyes and counted back from ten. "Sorry to interrupt your ill-advised jaunt around the village, but I can't find the Wi-Fi password. I was wondering if you had it written down somewhere."

"What was that?"

"The internet password."

"Speak up darling, you tend to mumble."

Ten...nine...eight...seven...

"Mom, can you please just—"

"Sweetheart, you're an international spy. You travel around the globe shooting people full of neurotoxins and breaking into security vaults. You really can't figure out the Wi-Fi password?"

The line went dead.

Molly clutched the phone in her hand. She counted backward from ten once more. Then she pressed her face into one of the gilded throw pillows, and screamed as loud as she could.

She surfaced a moment later, breathing hard.

No matter, I have people for that.

She tried calling her father, but apparently there wasn't a signal on the *windswept moors*. She tried calling Luke, but it went straight to voicemail because he was teaching a class. Without really thinking it through, she dialed a restricted number to contact Guilder tech-support.

You can hack anything, right? I'm sure they can break into my mom's—

A deep voice entered the line.

"Code in, please."

In a rush of panic, she hung up the phone.

Can't. Too humiliating.

The frenzy waned a moment and she stood in the middle of the floor—an island in the storm, forcing a careful calm. There was no reason she had to stay in the house. She had come to care for her mother, but her mother had left. There was no reason she couldn't do the same.

In a flash, she grabbed her purse from the coffee table and slipped on her shoes, striding out the door and down the garden path. The rain had stopped and the sky was beautiful, nothing more than a bright-eyed memory of the howling winds that had come before.

She set off walking with no actual purpose or destination. For those first few minutes, it was enough simply not to be in the house. The streets were paved in stone instead of asphalt. All the houses clung to the edges in a tidy line. By the time it began to dawn on her that the town was small and she couldn't walk forever, she stumbled right into the very place she would have chosen to go.

Coffee and internet.

Her face warmed with a smile.

I may apply for a job.

She pushed open the door, shivering involuntarily as a burst from the churning heaters flushed her icy cheeks. The hoodie came off immediately and she breathed in the familiar aroma of sugared pastries and espresso-scented steam. Instead of quickening in anticipation, her pulse actually slowed with a sudden lull of calm. She was safe now, the crisis was over. She had found the hive.

Still smiling to herself, she waltzed up to the counter, ordered the largest coffee money could buy, then settled herself at a table by the window—reaching into her purse and pulling out the bridal magazines she'd purchased at the airport. While she may have technically been married already, she continued to reach for them like an addict. And besides, weddings were a frequent source of conversation in those days. Ever since London's favorite assassin proposed to a ballerina bride.

I wonder if we should do a theme wedding, incorporate one of Natasha's favorite ballets...

When Gabriel had announced he wanted a big wedding—a declaration that made some of the friends balk in surprise, and the others roll their eyes in exasperation—it had only taken a short amount of time for the he's and she's to become a collective *we*.

Molly remembered the moment like yesterday. She played it often in her mind.

He had asked her to meet him at a café, only a few days after he'd popped the question. The agency was still in shock, the city was still in a state of disrepair, and it was the first time any of them had really left the house since that fateful day. He didn't mince words. He got right to the point.

"I love this girl more than life."

Molly nodded quickly.

"She deserves perfection."

Another nod.

"So will you plan the wedding?"

Despite all their battles and missions, all the death threats and drunken evenings and that tricky week they got trapped back in time, the pair had never embraced quite like they did that day.

It was enough to make Gabriel stumble. *Gabriel* who never stumbled. It was enough to make Molly leap off the table and cling to him like a child, tears of silent joy running down her cheeks.

Giselle's a little dark, but I love some of the costuming...

She slurped happily on her drink, thumbing through the magazines and pausing every so often with either the brightest smile or a disapproving scowl. There was a fine line between elegance and indulgence, between innovation and crime. In her years of relentless study, she'd learned to navigate those lines well. And one of her favorite pastimes was to bestow that advice upon others.

She was so consumed with the task, gleefully debating between waistlines and wondering if Natasha would consent to wear yet another tiara even though it would be her day off work, that she didn't notice the band of young women walking up the street until they'd already spotted her.

There was a collective gasp, some uncivilized pointing, then they raced inside with matching smiles, setting up a casual surveillance on the opposite side of the coffee shop. She glimpsed them only when they were settled, stiffening involuntarily, before letting out a quiet sigh.

She had met these people before. Many times.

Like most towns of a miniscule size, there was a massive exodus amongst the young people when they came of age. But like most towns of a miniscule size, there was always an inexplicable percentage of the population that stayed. Those ones were dug in for life, their roots buried in the very foundations. And despite being fortified with a heavy sense of belonging, they shared another commonality that hobbled them every step of the way. They were intensely, unendingly bored.

When Molly had first visited the town, fresh from her opening semester at Guilder, she had been the shiniest novelty to which any of them could aspire. They'd reached out immediately, made a semi-successful attempt to make friends. But gossip in a small town was like blood to vampires.

She was friendly, but detached. Mysterious. Something to unravel.

When she came back a few years later with an equally mysterious young man, a dark-haired beauty she insisted was only a friend, the intrigue deepened. When she came back a few years after that with a diamond and a child, having married one of the most shockingly attractive men any of them had ever seen, she became something of a legend. Now she was back again. Alone. Interesting.

Bloody hell.

When their staring became too obvious, she lifted a reluctant hand in a wave, flashing a tight smile. It was returned with such aggressive enthusiasm that the trained operative in her was tempted to reach for her gun. But there was little point. These people were dangerous in other ways.

And they were already heading her way.

"Molly?" The girl in front flashed a blinding smile, taking in every inch of her with a sweep of the eyes. "We thought that was you! It's so good to see you! When did you get into town?"

Molly stood up with a forced smile, allowing herself to be passed around the friends group in a series of awkward hugs, before clinging again to the safety of her chair.

"Only last night, actually. My mom had this surgery—"

"Oh, my goodness—we heard!" A blonde with springy curls rubbed her back in a way that was meant to be comforting, sinking uninvited into the adjacent chair. "It was her hip, right? The whole town was rooting for her. How did everything go?"

Molly froze a split second, trying to remember her name.

Isla. Isla Louise Aikens knew my mother was having surgery.

But I never got a call.

She stared a split second, before flashing another quick smile.

"It went fine. Everything's fine." She blinked. "Wait. It was her knee, not hip. She's still fine." She shifted uncomfortably beneath their ravenous gaze.

These people would not settle for fine. They wanted details. They wanted drama. If she was in a better state of mind, she might have actually played along, had a little fun with it. But as things stood, she wanted nothing more than to drink her coffee, drool over dresses, and be left alone.

As they began chattering excitedly back and forth, she took her phone and slid it discreetly beneath the table—nodding along obediently, as she searched for the correct button.

There was a loud vibration and she pretended to startle.

"Oh, I'm so sorry. I have to take this."

They stepped backward at the same time, like an apologetic flock of birds. *Oh, of course*, they crooned. *Do whatever you have to*. Then her favorite: *We'll be right over there if you need to talk.*

She thanked them profusely, bestowed a few quick parting hugs. She even complimented the springy blonde one's hair. Then she pressed a button on speed dial, fluttering her fingers in farewell.

The phone rang twice, then the line opened.

"Hello?"

She picked up her coffee, leaning back with a bright smile.

"*Hello* there! And how's my favorite groom-to-be?"

A spattering of gunfire echoed in the background, followed by a few large explosions. He sprinted to better cover, somersaulted behind it, then cupped a hand over his ear.

"Sorry, Molls. What was that?"

She flashed a quick look at the receiver. "...is this a bad time?"

It wasn't really a fair question.

Gabriel didn't know if it was a bad time. He didn't have those knee-jerk answers like other people. He'd been raised in an evil melting pot where all those lines blended together. Where they interrogated people in the same bathroom where they brushed their teeth and cut their hair.

Was it a bad time? Of course it was.

But Gabriel took the call anyway.

"I've got a minute. How's mommy-dearest?"

She rolled her eyes, wondering if she should begin the story with the feed cart, or jump straight into the crêpes. In the end, she decided to do neither and focus on something happy instead.

"Oh, you know...same battle, different day." She leaned forward with sudden excitement, tapping her fingers on the magazine. "I was actually hoping to have a little wedding chat."

"Ah, I see."

There was another explosion, followed by a series of screams. Gabriel peered out from behind a corner—hovering the phone with his tatù, so both hands were free to hold his gun.

Molly heard the metallic click, instantly determining the brand and caliber. "Where are you?"

He fired off three shots, then pressed his back against the wall. "I'm trying to get into that new Thai place by the park. The place is packed."

She nodded absentmindedly, flipping through the pages. "So, what do you think about hiring a sketch artist for the reception, instead of a photobooth? We could even get one of those guys who do caricatures. We'd have to vet him first."

"I think our friends drink a lot," he panted in reply.

She frowned at the phone. "What's that supposed to mean?"

"It means, our friends drink a lot. You want to get them drunk, then hire some unsuspecting guy to get them all together and point out their flaws?" He jerked his head as a bullet buried into the stone wall just beside him. "Do we later chase the man around with sticks? Venting our rage?"

Molly stared out the window, shaking her head. "Your sister would love that."

"That's a *no* to the caricature artist."

"Right," she agreed immediately, "but it's a maybe for the sketch artist? I mean, we could always go the conventional route and have Julian look ahead and paint them now. But some girls might not have decided what they want to wear yet, so we couldn't give them away as gifts."

He cast the phone a sideways glance. "You already know what you're wearing to my wedding?"

"I got a vague sense of it the day we met." She flipped to a pre-bookmarked page. "Okay then, last thing for today. I want you to look at table settings—not what's actually included, but just the general shape. I'm going to flash two pictures, you tell me which one you like best."

She came to a sudden pause. "There *is* a right answer to this, Gabriel. So give it some thought."

There was a deafening crash, followed by the shattering of glass.

"You're going to flash two pictures?" he repeated breathlessly.

"Yeah, can you facetime for a second?"

A series of bombs went off in the distance, throwing him out the open window and onto the cratered street. She took another sip of coffee, wondering if she should have gotten cream.

"I'm kind of pinned down by this separatist group—"

"And I'm trying to avoid the local gossip-hounds," she whispered, cupping a hand over the receiver. "We've all got problems today, Alden. Work with me."

He hesitated only a moment, then lobbed a grenade over his shoulder.

"Alright, I've got a little time." He ducked for the subsequent explosion. "Invite me."

She leaned back and switched the call to video, giving him a cheerful wave, before propping the screen up against the salt shaker and lifting the magazine instead. She took a second to find the correct pictures, then covered them quickly so he wasn't able to see.

"This is going to be fast, okay? Think carefully, but I want a gut reaction."

"Makes perfect sense."

She flashed the magazine for a split second, then clutched it back to her chest. There was a moment of silence, as her knees bounced impatiently beneath the table. Another moment went by.

"Gabriel?"

"I think you froze."

Typical.

"Alright, I'm doing it again." She opened the magazine again, unaware that her performance was beginning to attract attention. "Which one do you like better? Right or left?"

He shook his head uncertainly, squinting in the clouds of dust.

"It's, uh...it's a little hard to tell. We're going to do this when I get back, alright?"

What—no!

"What—no!"

Never one to filter her thoughts, Molly banged her hand against the table—staring into the screen with an expression that was as earnest as it was ridiculously grave.

"You need to pick something now. Because that will give me an idea as to the general style, and that's something I need to know before we start narrowing down the invitations, and *that* is something that should have happened four weeks ago. So you really need to pick something now!"

Gabriel stared down at the camera—coated in plaster, smudged in soot. A Bosnian village was collapsing behind him and from the sharp pain in his side, he was fairly sure he'd cracked a rib.

But for a fleeting moment, his lips curved with a little smile.

"...why does this matter so much to you?"

She pulled in a deep breath, speaking directly into the phone.

"Because you deserve happiness more than anyone I've ever met and *that's* what I'm going to give you, Gabriel Alden. This wedding...is going to be the happiest day you've ever known."

There was a stifled gasp and she glanced up to see five sets of eyes shoot away at the same time. The phones were already out and their fingers were flying. Another layer of intrigue, another mysterious man. Not the husband. Not the 'platonic' love interest. And the wedding...?!

I should have brewed coffee at the house.

MOLLY FLED THE CAFÉ almost immediately after and wandered the town for a while before eventually trudging back to the house. Her mother arrived at the same time from the other direction.

Both looked completely exhausted. Both were quick to smile.

"How was your walk?" Molly asked.

"It was fine. How was your coffee?" Eleanor's eyes swept her up and down, lingering on the jittery fingers and caffeinated flush to her cheeks. "I heard you put on a little show."

Already? This place is worse than Guilder!

Molly squared her shoulders, refusing to give anything away. "I ran into some of the local girls. They made some...assumptions."

Her mother nodded slowly, never breaking her gaze. "They were probably wondering why you didn't come with your husband."

Husband. Molly clenched her jaw in silence. *She won't even say his name.*

To put things incredibly lightly, Eleanor didn't care for Luke.

She'd *loved* him at first. It was impossible not to love him. Even his sociopathic older brother and militaristic father eventually had to give in. But then she'd learned his story. Then she'd found out that his father operated yet another international organization of supernatural spies.

She'd never gotten over it.

It didn't matter how kind he was, or how many favors he performed, or how many pictures of Benji he sent in a shameless attempt to win her affection. It didn't matter how wildly, unspeakably happy he made her only daughter. It was over before it even had a chance to begin.

Coincidentally, Eleanor didn't like Rae for the same reason. She was the embodiment of all things magic. It was bad enough her own daughter could shoot lightning out of her hands.

"You can't blame them for being curious," Eleanor continued lightly, flashing a look over her shoulder as she stepped through the door. "I always wished you'd married the dark-haired one."

Molly sighed quietly, walking inside behind her. "I know, Mom."

Chapter 6

The next day started on a positive note.

"On behalf of the general public, we must find you something civilized to wear."

Molly glanced up from her breakfast cereal, wearing the same outfit she'd travelled in two days before. She'd attempted a late-night washing, only to discover she had no earthly idea how to use the machine. Too embarrassed to ask, she'd scrubbed the clothes for a while in the sink, then put them on that morning wrinkled and damp—hoping they'd escape those hawkish eyes.

"Yeah, I wasn't..." She trailed off, wondering how to finish the sentence. "To be honest, I was thinking the same thing."

I might have said it nicer.

"There's a new boutique at the far end of town, right across from the nail salon." Eleanor wiped her mouth on a stiff napkin and stood up from the table. "We can go right after you change."

Molly glanced at her half-eaten bowl of cereal, then seemed to realize she was finished. "After I change?" she repeated. "I told you, the airline lost all my bags."

"And I understand that. But what *you* must understand, is that as your mother, I simply cannot allow you to be seen wearing that outside the house. It's for your own good, darling."

Darling.

Molly had grown to hate the word. "I don't have anything else here," she said flatly.

Her mother stared her down with a smile, that slice of a frame pointing like an arrow straight toward the ceiling. "Which is why I'm lending you something of mine," she explained with irritating patience. "Run along, now—chop, chop. And try to remember, you're a winter, not a spring."

Molly stared at her a moment, then pushed robotically to her feet and headed for the stairs.

Ten...nine...eight...seven...

At this point, it was getting counterproductive. It was starting to sound like a countdown.

On a nuclear clock.

There was nothing particularly sentimental about Molly's room in the house. Mostly because, it didn't feel like her room. She hadn't spent much time there—her folks had moved from Wales just as she'd started her second year living in the Guilder dorms. They hadn't made a big announcement and she didn't find out until Christmas, and to be honest, it never bothered her. Home was Guilder at that point. Most of her things from the old house had moved to England with her. Whatever was left, had been packed into boxes. The place where she was sleeping now felt no more sentimental than an overpriced hotel. But her mother's room...?

That was a different story.

The first thing that hit her was the smell. A sharp tang that was hard to identify, mixed with something fainter and sweeter. Licorice, maybe. She had never been able to tell. Her eyes closed and she sucked in a deep breath, letting it fill every corner. The memories hit a second later.

Paperclip tiaras and carving pumpkins by firelight. A wooden rocking horse with magic marker scribbled on the sides. They seemed so distant now, so achingly removed, that she half-believed she'd invented them. But there were other things, too. Trinkets and totems. Tangible proof that the little family had been happy once. That things were not always the way they were now.

With a faint smile, she crossed the room to her mother's vanity.

It was bigger than most, with a silver-tipped mirror and a handful of products arranged to clinical perfection. It looked more like a stage prop than the actual thing. But what humanized it were the pictures mounted along the sides. The frames were elegant, the faces were not.

There were dozens, more than dozens. All crammed together and overlapping in a messy, heartfelt collage. While the edges were neatly contained, the people were spilling forth—a happy medley of toothless grins and first place ribbons. Of tap shoes, and spaghetti-explosions, and rain-soaked fishing trips where her father was smiling, while the others huddled murderously in the tent.

In one picture she was five years old and chin-deep in a meadow, holding a stuffed duck she used to sleep with each night. In another, she was looking at the camera with an absurdly stoic expression, as though the piano teacher standing beside her was about to stab her in the back.

And...that's where they stop.

At first, she thought it was an oversight, a mistake of her own. Again and again, her eyes flashed over each of the frames, searching for anything she might have missed. After a few minutes, she stopped trying and stared blankly at her own reflection in the mirror.

There's nothing. It's like time stopped when I turned sixteen.

A strange stillness swept across her body, like she'd been caught by a sudden wind.

Then with the skill of someone who'd done it far too many times, she exhaled it with a single breath, forgetting so completely, that if you'd asked a moment later what had been troubling her, she'd have to think a moment before giving a reply.

She paced over to the closet, pulling out the first thing in reach. It was a dress, casual enough to be worn for errands, yet costly enough to make everyone else feel their own worth.

Vintage Eleanor.

She zipped up the back and pinched a little color into her cheeks—leaning closer to examine her reflection. There it was again, that scent. She rummaged through the line of bottles, then picked up the perfume and spritzed some without thinking onto her wrist. Licorice? Cherry blossom?

She'd never figure it out.

MOLLY JOGGED BACK DOWNSTAIRS, taking a spare jacket from the linen closet, then stopped in surprise at the entrance of the kitchen. Her mother was standing with her back turned, leaning over the medication, a glass of water on the counter beside her. She read quickly through the labels and tipped three different pills into her hand, swallowing them down with a sharp tilt of the head. At that point, Molly wished very much to have announced herself already, but before she could ease back into the hallway, Eleanor turned and saw her watching by the door.

The two locked eyes for a split second, then glanced away with a flush.

"I'm afraid my pain threshold isn't what it used to be," Eleanor confessed wryly, screwing the lids on the bottles before sweeping her daughter with a practiced eye. "That looks lovely, dear."

Molly blinked in surprise, giving the skirt a nervous smooth. "Oh...thank you."

Did that just happen?

Eleanor nodded curtly and picked up her crutches. "Far better than I was expecting."

And we're back.

She swept past with a brittle smile, pinching her daughter's cheeks for still more color on the way to the foyer. Molly jammed the sweatshirt over the dress, and followed her out the door.

"I CAN'T BELIEVE YOU brought that thing."

It was a ten-minute walk across the entire town of Evanton. That was ten minutes, if you stopped a while to look at the old church at the end of the lane. But upon her mother's suggestion, Molly drove them to the boutique. She worried as to the reason the entire way there.

"I don't know what you mean," she replied lightly, tugging reflexively on her hoodie as they rolled to a stop. "It's starting to grow on me."

...like fungus.

Eleanor muttered something to the same effect, then began extracting herself carefully from the car, clinging to the rails and swatting herself free when Molly hurried to help her.

"It's fine," she snapped. "Everything's *fine.*" She cast another glance at the blaring purple fabric, looking personally offended that it had come along for the ride. "You should put up your hair. Then at least it will look like you've been exercising...and lost your mind."

Molly stopped in the middle of the sidewalk, speaking in a loud voice. "I don't know what you mean, mother. I think the hoodie is delightful." She turned around with a deadpan stare. "It brings out the color of my lovely eyes."

A few pedestrians glanced over as Eleanor pursed her lips with a hidden smile.

"Of course it does, darling." She patted her daughter firmly on the cheeks. "And I want you to keep telling yourself that every time you look in a mirror."

That's it—I'm heading for the embassy.

Molly forced a smile in return, then gestured to the shop. "Shall we?"

It was probably the only place in town that didn't have a little bell above the door to announce the arrival of customers. That was probably a large part of the reason that Eleanor had selected it. She approached things like shopping the way others strategized before a war. Spread out to cover the most distance, minimize exposure by making a surgical strike.

Take no prisoners.

"Alright, we'll need to start with a few of the basics," she instructed, nodding politely to the clerk as they made their way inside. "Skirts, blouses, and hosiery."

Molly snorted under her breath. "Hosiery," she repeated. "What century is this?"

Eleanor turned sharply, forcing her to stop. "Did you say something, Molly?"

There was a pause.

"No, ma'am."

They paced toward the back of the store, then drifted to opposite corners—thumbing through the racks and shelving, pulling out random pieces to either consider or discard. Oddly enough, this was a part of the excursion they did together—holding things up for the other's opinion before deciding whether to place them into the basket or not.

"You cannot be serious," Eleanor chided as her daughter held up a jacket. "Look at the stitchwork along the hem. The war has ended, sweetheart. I believe we can do better."

Molly slipped it back on the hanger, then whipped out another with a wicked smile.

"What about this?" she asked innocently, holding the orange pleating to her chest. "I could pair it with some leggings. Stand on the cliffs and warn the ships to keep away from shore."

Her mother chuckled, taking a bottle of sanitizer from her purse. "Put that back in the hellscape where you found it, and wash your hands."

They continued browsing for a while in companionable silence, slowly filling up the baskets draped over their arms. It was one of the things they did best together. Judgement and discovery, fashion at the core. Distant as they'd become, they'd been raised on the same magazines, revered the same designers, felt that aesthetic tick of things deep in their blood. In the last ten years, Eleanor had visited her daughter in London precisely once, and they'd spent the entire time at Harrods.

"So I guess the real question is...how long are you staying?" Eleanor picked up a pair of leather slacks, squinting at the hems. "Your father may have conscripted you into service, but I know there's a life waiting for you back in London. You probably can't wait to get home."

Molly shot a quick look across the store, hiding behind a pair of designer sunglasses. "I'm happy to stay as long as you need," she answered lightly. "At least until Dad gets back from his little pioneer reenactment. Heaven forbid you're up and walking around..."

Her mother continued browsing, keeping her eyes on the clothes. "Work can spare you, then? Not too busy?"

For the second time, Molly stopped cold.

Her mother didn't ask about her job. Not once. Not ever. When it became clear that job involved running around the world with superpowers and guns, that part of her daughter's life was excised forever—cut out like a diseased limb, before it could infect the surrounding flesh.

She considered a split second, then decided to ease them forward.

"Things are busy, but not really with work. A friend of mine is actually getting married in a few weeks. He asked me to plan the wedding."

Eleanor's head popped up behind a mirror. "Oh, yes?"

There was a pause.

"Have you decided on a theme?"

It was the perfect thing to say. Like a pair of lionesses on the hunt, that question led to another, which led to another, which carried them through the entire trip. The shopping was easier, the conversation was no longer forced. By the time they made their way up to the counter, dragging an extra three baskets of clothes, Molly could swear they were actually having a bit of fun.

"—which is why I told him that we should stick to silvers, instead of a slate grey. But of course, that's when it started raining and part of the sugar palace fell down."

Eleanor chuckled appreciatively, swatting down her daughter's credit card and replacing it with her own. The cashier rang them up, wrapping each item carefully in tissue paper, before folding it into a bag. They were going through her stock. She'd have to send out for more.

"It reminds me of the time your father announced that he wanted a snow wedding. It was a regular weekday morning, we were sitting down for a lovely brunch. Then he hits me with that."

Molly turned with a frown. "You mean like...a Christmas wedding?"

"That's how I interpreted it as well," Eleanor replied, shaking her head when the salesgirl attempted to ply them with more tissue paper. "But your father has always been quite literal. He wanted to get married in the middle of summer, in a place that was still coated in snow."

Bless his heart.

Molly laughed aloud, unable to help herself. "That sounds like Dad. How did you stop him?"

Her mother shrugged, adding a tube of lipstick to the pile. "I did what I always do. I frightened him with threats of mass hysteria and death." When the cashier slowly lifted her eyes, she graciously continued, "I told him that I wanted doves, and they freeze above a certain elevation. The man was so mortified by the visual, he never mentioned the snow again."

Molly nodded knowingly, looping a pair of bags around her wrist. "I once told Luke that ice-skating was linked to dementia, just so he wouldn't make me go."

Eleanor arched her eyebrows. "And he believed that? Rather gullible."

Molly bristled defensively. "He's trusting."

Come to think of it, that probably makes him a terrible spy.

"Sounds rather gullible to me." Eleanor turned back to the salesgirl, gesturing around the store. "You can tell Simone that I fully approve of the new shipment. She's really been taking those weekly lunches of ours to heart."

Molly bit her lip and stared out the window.

"Sure—will do," the girl replied. "These are some great leggings," she added as she folded them. "If you're interested in some bolder colors, we've actually got a spandex version..."

She trailed off, as both women gave her the same imperial scowl.

"...I'll just carry the rest out to your car."

DURING THE DRIVE BACK home, they were still talking. The windows fogged from the constant conversation and they stopped at a deli to pick up sandwiches for lunch. This time, Molly moved quickly enough that she was able to pay. It was an absolute novelty. Not until that very moment, did she realize that her mother had never allowed her to buy anything in proximity her entire life.

"Would you like to get manicures?" she offered, riding the high "My treat."

Her eyes flicked down to her mother's legs and she decided against suggesting a pedicure. The woman was so skilled at hiding her limp, she wasn't even sure which knee had been surgically replaced. She might have asked, but her mother was equally deft at dodging conversation. She also tried to avoid the crutches as much as she could. Even had a cane in the car to use instead.

Eleanor's eyes flitted to the salon before she headed back to the car. "Let's just take the sandwiches home. You look worn out."

Molly glanced up in surprise and started the car, eyes drifting once more to her mother's knees. "Yeah, I am a little. We'll be there in three."

She drove much quicker than was wise in a town with a single neighborhood policeman. By now the man was so bored, he might have constructed a public gallows as punishment just to have something to do. They rolled to a stop on the gravel, and it took everything Molly had not to circle around the car and help her mother down. She kept careful watch instead, always ready with a hand.

Is this how it's going to be as they both get older? Who will be there to do this, when I live so far away?

"There's a pitcher of iced tea in the refrigerator," Eleanor directed, as they stepped inside and headed for the kitchen. "You get that out—I'll put these on plates."

It didn't matter if it was a box of doughnuts or Chinese noodles, there were no take-out containers in the house. Food would be 'properly plated' the moment it arrived, so they could sit down and eat like a 'civilized family.' A family whose mother could 'cook.'

Molly saluted sarcastically and followed obediently behind her, retrieving the drink and the glasses, while her mother unrolled the wax paper and set the sandwiches on the plates. The bags were left unceremoniously in the middle of the hallway. It had always been the one exception to the otherwise clinical perfection of the house. If you went shopping, you were allowed to leave a mess.

"So how did you get here again?" Eleanor begin with a frown, kissing a bit of oil from her finger as she reached for the napkins. "Some man picked you up in the back of his truck?"

Hardly the riskiest thing I've done this month.

"He was an ancient farmer," Molly replied lightly. "Had to have been around nine hundred years old, with just enough jowls to hide his forked tongue. He lied to me about the potholes."

Eleanor laughed shortly, picking up the plates. "You're lucky the road was paved at all," she answered, carrying them to the table. "Most of the lanes around these parts got washed away by the—"

There was a sharp gasp as her knee gave way beneath her, pitching her forward onto the marble tile. The plates flew from her hands at the same time, landing with a mighty clatter and rocketing across the floor. Splashes of condiments and pieces of lettuce misted into the air in a culinary explosion, but were instantly forgotten as Eleanor let out a muffled cry of pain.

There was no move to get up. She simply clutched her knee, white as a sheet.

"Mom!"

Molly had frozen the second it happened, watching with wide eyes from across the room, but she was racing forward before the plates even stopped moving—dropping immediately to the floor by the mother's side. Two hands came up to balance her, but they were instantly pushed away.

"Don't coddle me," Eleanor snapped, panting for breath. "It's this damn bandage they taped beneath the brace. Sometimes the two get caught—"

"Be quiet."

Her mother froze with an expression Molly would always have remembered, if she had taken the time to look. But the second she hit the floor, the dynamics that usually governed them faded, and over a decade's worth of training sprang up to take its place.

Despite her mother's protests, she anchored the leg calmly beneath her own and gently rolled up pants until they were above the wound. She'd been right. The brace she was wearing—so slim, Molly hadn't even known it was there—had gotten caught on the thick bandage and pulled itself askew. The skin beneath was pale and stained with old bruises. A knot lodged in Molly's throat.

"We shouldn't have gone out today," she muttered.

Eleanor glanced up swiftly, still trying to recover from the shock. "They said walking is vital for my recovery—"

"Not that much," Molly interrupted quietly. "Lean back."

Her mother blanched, leaning away from her hands. "What are you doing?" she demanded. "We need to call the doctor, Molly. This happened already once with your father. They made us drive all the way back to Inverness—"

Snap.

The splint burst open and Eleanor froze utterly still, staring with a look of true astonishment at her daughter's face. For a split second, it broadened to include something more. A flicker of curiosity. A note of pride. A second later, they were gone—vanishing like smoke on the air.

"You don't get squeamish," she remarked, wincing involuntarily as Molly peeled back the bandage still further, checking on the integrity of the wound. "Perhaps that time bumping around in the straw did you good."

Molly's lips twitched, though she didn't quite smile. She was still bent over the crooked splint, feeling it up and down to find the correct pressure. There were a few seconds when nothing happened, then all at once, her face lightened with recognition and she slid it into place.

"There—how's that?"

Her mother rotated it hesitantly at first, then all at once. "It's good. *Very* good." Her eyes sharpened with sudden intensity, sweeping over every inch of her daughter's face. "You've done something like this before."

Usually, Molly would deny it. Usually, she would make up some excuse.

But they'd gotten leggings and sandwiches. They'd laughed in the car.

"On a prison raid, in Algeria." She spoke quietly, keeping her eyes on the floor. "One of the locals got hit by shrapnel. I helped the village midwife to set his leg."

Time slowed and the room went abruptly quiet—quiet enough that she could hear each of her mother's shallow breaths. Quiet enough that she could hear the moment they stopped.

"Forget the sandwiches." Eleanor pushed to her feet, limping from the room. "I've lost my appetite."

Molly crouched like a statue on the floor, rigid with surprise and delayed bursts of adrenaline as her heart pounded in her chest. It took a while to slow back down, for things to steady, but she had a while. The kitchen was empty. Her mother would not be returning.

She took one breath, then another. Then she reached into her pocket and pulled out her phone. The number was already waiting and she texted without looking, tears rolling down her face.

It was a mistake, coming here. A horrible mistake.

Chapter 7

Molly woke up the next morning to a knock on the door. She hadn't slept in her bedroom, though she wasn't exactly sure of the reason. Instead of venturing up that looming stairwell, she curled up on the living room couch. She peeled her face slowly off the ornate pillow, a strange cluster of patterns imprinted into her cheek. The sky was a budding pink, just barely touched by the sun's light. But she could have sworn there was a knock.

With a flutter of sleepy curiosity, she wrapped a blanket around her shoulders and padded down the hallway, passing the mess of condiments still smeared across the kitchen floor. She hadn't had the heart yesterday to clean them. She'd gotten as far as pulling out a towel, before throwing it against the dishwasher and silently weeping right there on the floor. Her throat tightened again as she walked past it, pulsing with a raw ache, like she'd spent the night screaming instead.

She tried to push past it. She cleared her face and opened the door. Then her breath caught in her chest.

"I got your text."

Julian.

There he was just like magic. Five hundred miles from home, but standing on the porch like it was the most natural thing in the world. He was holding a coffee in one hand and a Prada handbag in the other. He extended both with a little smile, curls of mist rising off the shoulders of his coat.

"Rae said the airline lost your bags."

Molly stood there a second longer, as if a tiny part of her wasn't convinced it was real. Then she flung herself upon him—colliding with such violence, he needed to take a quick step back.

"She's right," she breathed, pressing her face into his shirt. "I should have married you."

He lifted his eyebrows, holding her close. "What?"

She just hugged him tighter, grinning all the while.

Her life had changed a great deal since moving to England—filling to the brim with such a constant stream of fantastical novelty, it bore little resemblance to the way it was at the start. There were changes in rhythm, changes in expectation. Changes in the way she began to think of herself and imagine different versions of the way her life might play out. Truth be told, it wasn't the school, or the tatù, or the occasional cataclysmic disasters that set it so far apart. It was the people.

Never in her life could she have imagined such people.

If asked to describe them, most people would leap for the extremes. They were dangerous, they were unprecedented. They were heroes. They had been called "high-spirited" more than once.

But if she had to pin them down with a single word, it would be unlikely.

There was no plausible reason for why a group of such different people would have grown into family. Their stories had started in such wildly contrasting places, the way they'd fit themselves together seemed the most improbable thing of all. Everything they'd done before, merely set them on the path. Everything they'd done after, was a direct conse-quence of that unlikely, infallible bond.

In the years that followed, they had seen each other through all the rest.

Funerals and pregnancies. Bad haircuts and moments of apocalyp-tic shock. They had discovered a world of magic, then sacrificed every-thing they had to protect it. They had fallen off the ledge and dragged each other back time, after time, after time. They had married each other, cared for each other. They had challenged and chided each other. Set goals and made plans.

But there were certain moments in Molly's life—moments when she felt so lost, it seemed like she might never recover—when she would only ever call for one of them.

"She's suffocating me," she whispered into his dark hair. "She's stamping out my life."

He squeezed her tighter, lifting her toes off the ground. "We'll fight her together."

There was movement inside the house, a distant creaking on the stairs. The pair detached themselves, glancing over their shoulders just as the woman of the hour swept down the hall.

"Why do I hear male voices?" she called ahead, rounding the corner. "There had better not be any—" She stopped in her tracks. "Oh—Julian! How very good to see you!"

He stepped forward with a smile, pressing a kiss to her cheek. "It's good to see you too, Mrs. Skye. Sorry for dropping by unannounced."

Most people would have corrected him. *Please, call me Eleanor.* That sort of thing. But while Mrs. Skye liked Julian very much—she wasn't most people.

"Nonsense," she declared, stepping back to look at him, "we're happy to have you."

Molly looked back and forth between them with a giddy smile, feeling about three hundred pounds lighter. The mere proximity was already doing wonders—placing things back into context and lifting her out of the fog. This wasn't going to last forever. They'd only linger a few more days.

Then she played back the last few sentences in her head.

"Male voices," she repeated. "Plural? There's just the two of us."

Eleanor gave her a quick squeeze, eyes still locked on their guest. "You've always had a very androgynous voice, sweetheart."

Julian bowed his head, while Molly flushed a murderous shade of red.

"As you're so fond of telling me..."

"Come inside." Her mother ignored this like she did everything, taking the psychic's arm and escorting him through the door. "I'll get changed, then whip you up something to eat."

UNLIKE THE OTHERS, Julian had actually been to the house before. When they were teenagers, still at school, he'd often stayed with Devon during the holidays, but he'd flown over once for Christmas when Molly needed moral support. He'd come again the next summer, helping her unpack a few of those boxes, squeezing her hand beneath the table whenever things got rough.

The glorious thing about Julian was that he was just as impossible to hate as Luke. But while her husband was crippled by heritage, the psychic had two things going for him: he wasn't the heir to a supernatural agency, and he wasn't trying to sleep with anyone's daughter.

At any rate...Eleanor didn't exactly know he was psychic.

Perhaps she was acting in her own self-interest, but Molly had never been quite honest about Julian (though in her defense, he was a little hard to explain). When asked why he attended the same school as the rest, she'd replied with a vague, "Jules gets a sense for things," and left it at that.

If Eleanor Beatrice Skye were ever to witness a full-on clairvoyant transformation, to see his face awash in prophetic light, she'd probably drive him back to the border herself.

He followed obediently inside, Molly shadowing behind him.

"Did you get a new coffee table?"

He always noticed things like that—changes in curtains and furniture, faces missing from pictures and the things that made people smile.

He could sit with endless patience at the table, listening to her mother prattle on about things he didn't care about and people he didn't know.

He remembered every word of it. He'd mention specific details next time he arrived.

"Yes, it is, darling boy," Eleanor called over her shoulder, marching up the stairs. "We got it at an auction in Paris last spring. Make yourself at home—I'll be down shortly."

He waited until she was gone, then turned to Molly, offering out the coffee.

Only then did she realize, it was from her favorite café back in London—the place she always went when Rae was away from the city and couldn't conjure things herself. The purse was no doubt stuffed with similar goodies, just like the messenger bag slung across his back.

Her face lit up in delight, as she took it from his hands.

"Seriously?" she asked in wonder. "How did you possibly bring that all the way here?"

"I've reheated it nine times."

She took a sip, then spat it discreetly back into the cup. "The cream's gone sour."

He nodded sadly. "There was a good chance of that happening."

They stared at each other, then embraced again.

This one felt different from the first. He was there now. It was firm and concrete. She drew in a deep breath, curling her fingers around the jacket and drinking in the scent of him. The worst was already behind her. There was safety in numbers. At least more safety than there was before.

"Come on." He tilted his head toward the kitchen. "I'll make a pot."

In hindsight, it was probably the kind of thing she should have done herself. The man had left his family and stranded himself in the Scottish Highlands, the least she could do was play hostess and make him something to drink. But her brain was still fuzzy with relief, and at any rate, Julian didn't seem to mind. He had come there to help. That was exactly what he intended to do.

After casting a quick look around the kitchen, one his vivacious friend never got to see, he stepped casually over the remains of the sandwiches and started up the brew. He then picked up the same towel Molly had thrown the night before, and started mopping up the mess.

"I can do that," she murmured hastily, flushing with shame. "Give me the—"

"Open the bag."

She paused for a moment, then looked at the purse he'd placed upon the counter.

He must have felt ridiculous carrying it through two separate airports, but after what had happened the last time, he didn't want to risk checking anything himself. Mechanical failures and baggage overflow weren't premeditated decisions, and he was at the same mercies as anyone else.

She popped open the clasps, then looked inside with a grin.

He hadn't packed her clothes or toiletries. Nothing that might be of any practical use. He'd brought her pillow from home. The one she had trouble sleeping without.

"Thanks, Jules."

He straightened up with a smile, tossing the towel into the sink.

"A woman on the plane loved it—said I was very brave." His lips curved in amusement, before he glanced up with a sudden frown. "She also called it a clutch. But I thought—"

"It's *not* a clutch," Molly interrupted emphatically, "it's a *purse*. Who are these random women spreading disinformation to strangers on planes? I'm telling you, Julian, if these kinds of things were up to me, there would never—"

"Ah—I see you're making yourself right at home." Eleanor swept around the corner with a smile, wearing a blazer that had been starched to such a degree, it made an almost clicking sound when she walked.

She glanced into the bag as she passed, and gave his arm a quick squeeze. "We do have pillows in the house, Julian, but I appreciate you bringing one just in case."

He flashed a grin, leaning into those boyish charms. "You can never be too careful. We are in *Scotland*, after all."

She swatted him with a dishrag.

"Crosswords, huh?" he continued, spotting the one she'd brought with her. "Is it a hobby, or an obsession? I've heard people fall into one of two camps."

"It's a *distraction*, from the daily horror of my life." Her eyes lifted with a wry sparkle, locking on her daughter. "Tell me, Julian. What's a seven-letter word for a burden one delivers?"

His expression froze, while Molly glanced up with a sweet smile.

"Some people do these things in ink. My mother does them in blood."

This is where he regrets coming to Scotland.

He took a beat, but recovered quickly—fetching down another pair of mugs and filling the kettle for tea. "I'd guess *the news*, but that might be an over-simplification."

There was a genuine burst of laughter, as things eased forward again.

Considering he never had parents of his own, Julian was a natural. Blame it on his time spent in an orphanage, blame it on the subsequent years balancing life as a spy, but he'd developed a keen instinct for pleasing people in positions of authority, for knowing the perfect thing to say.

He always took precisely the right amount of crêpes.

"Have you eaten already?" Eleanor called over her shoulder, pulling a tin of biscuits down from the shelf and arranging them deftly on a plate. "We were just getting up ourselves."

"I can eat again, thank you." He sat down at the table, shaking his hair from his eyes. "I hate to fly so early in the morning. I'd rather stay up late."

Eleanor nodded approvingly, setting down a jar of honey. "Pull back your hair, dear."

He flashed Molly a quick look, then complied with a little smile, knotting it behind his head as she settled across from them and presented the biscuits.

"There, that's rather fetching." She gestured to the plates, signaling them to begin. "Well, by now, I'm sure you've heard the entire sordid tale from Molly—but I'll tell it again. I was out in the garden, doing heaven knows what—who can remember, when my boot caught the edge of an old fence post and I found myself face-down in the dirt. Terribly undignified. I was discovered a few hours later by the gardeners. There was quite a bit of pain, as well. It'd been sore and had issues for quite a while, but that was the breaking point, I guess."

Molly froze in her chair, staring with wide eyes across the table. Her father had been brief on the phone, and her mother had volunteered no details. After their little mishap the previous evening, she'd resigned herself never to ask. Truth be told, she didn't know why her mother was sharing now.

Julian read his friend's face, then prodded with gentle questions.

"I'm so sorry," he murmured, taking a biscuit off the tray. "The same thing happened to a cousin of mine—he got nicked by a delivery truck, had to get the same surgery. They kept him for observation a while. Were you only in the hospital the one night?"

Molly threw him a swift look, then held back a smile.

Her sweet, deceptive friend. The one who didn't have siblings, didn't have aunts or uncles, didn't even have parents, until a recent reunion with his dad. She'd heard of his "cousin" before.

Poor bloke has the worst luck.

"Two nights," Eleanor corrected, smearing a dollop of honey onto her plate. "But they say that's not to be unexpected. I'm assuming your cousin was quite young."

Julian nodded thoughtfully.

"They gave him some brutal physical therapy. Four mornings a week with a specialist on Harley Street. The insurance company made him drive all the way across town."

Those bastards.

"Mine's not quite as bad as all that," her mother replied, dabbing her lips with a napkin. "But I do have a session today, as fate would have it. Molly, can you drive me?"

Molly startled in surprise. At this point, she half-expected Julian to complete his martyrdom and do the honors himself. Only a few bites of breakfast and the two were already thick as thieves.

"Yeah, of course. Let me just get changed." She stood up quickly from the table, casting an apologetic look at her friend. "Jules, could you hang out here a few hours? There's tons of—"

"Don't get the boy's hopes up with books and movies," Eleanor interrupted, eyes twinkling with mischief. "I know how much a young father craves quiet and relaxation, but you're fresh out of luck, my dear, because you're not going to find that here. I have something else in mind for you."

"YOU CAN'T BE SERIOUS. You want him to fix the roof?"

Molly and Julian stood within arm's reach of each other, heads tilted at the same comical angle as they stared toward the top of the house. There was a cluster of loose tiles beneath the chimney, like an uprooted seam. The paths to get there were coated in a heavy layer of moss.

"Sweetheart, don't insult the man." Eleanor squinted upwards as well before planting her hands on her hips and turning to Julian. "I'm sure you've fixed a roof or two before?"

There was a beat of silence.

"...of course."

This from a boy who couldn't make pancakes.

"But if I'm stretching that a bit to appear likable," he quickly added, "is this the kind of thing where if I mess it up, the ceiling falls and kills you in your sleep?"

That's not exactly a deal-breaker.

"Of course not," she replied, "don't be ridiculous. There's a little tin of epoxy in the shed, you just dab and stick, dab and stick. The tiles themselves are purely cosmetic."

The friends shifted nervously, both facing the same dilemma. It didn't sound right, but neither of them knew enough about either tiles or epoxy to prove it was untrue.

Eleanor remained willfully oblivious, smearing on lipstick as she spoke. "Molly's father was going to do it before he left, but now he's off playing shepherd—silly little man—and I need it taken care of before the next time it rains. You don't mind, do you Julian?"

Molly threw up her hands. "He *minds*, Mom."

"Of course not," Julian said at the same time. He pressed a finger to Molly's lips before she could speak again, keeping his eyes on her mother. "Of course not."

Eleanor smirked triumphantly and waltzed off to the car.

They waited until she was gone, then turned back to each other. At that point, Molly bit the finger and lifted a choice one of her own, but he caught her just as quickly—forcing her into a hug.

"Go spend some time with your mom. I'll be just fine over here."

She bit him again for good measure, staring glumly over his shoulder. "Easy for you to say. I have to be within reach of those claws for probably an hour of physical therapy. When she's feeling defensive and exposed. All you have to do is fall off a roof."

His eyes twinkled and he pressed a kiss to her forehead. "You know I love you, right?"

She let out a sigh. "I love you, too."

Chapter 8

As it turned out, attending physical therapy with Eleanor Skye didn't turn into quite the catastrophic disaster that Molly had in mind. *Yes*, there were a few precarious moments involving an unsupervised defibrillator, and *yes*, a few of the nurses were looking at her with the same expression captives use when trying to pass messages of escape. But there was such a complete lack of *actual* bloodshed, that Molly couldn't help but count it as a grand success. By the time they pulled into the gravel driveway, she was ready to schedule the next appointment herself.

"I still can't believe you did that," she murmured as they rolled to a stop, staring through the windshield at Julian's perch upon the roof. "I still can't believe you made him go up there."

Eleanor leaned forward as well, enjoying the view. "What's the point of my daughter having strapping, young friends, if I can't take advantage from time to time? And, darling, let's be clear..."

She didn't finish. She didn't have to.

It may not have been very warm that time in Scotland, but the sun was out and Julian had been working hard. As the day progressed, he'd gradually peeled off the layers of his London wardrobe, until only a thin tank remained—damp from sweat and dusty with plaster. His dark hair was still tied back in a careless knot. Flashes of sunlight glinted off the lean muscles in his arms.

It was the kind of sight that still managed to make an impression, even when Molly had seen it a hundred times before. It was the same kind of sight that made people pause awkwardly on the sidewalk as they passed by, wondering about things like the price of apartment rentals in London.

Mother and daughter shared a grin, then stepped out of the car.

"Hello there!" Eleanor called out first, shielding her eyes from the sun. "I thought you might be done already. I'm so thrilled that you're not. How's it going up there?"

Julian caught sight of them at the same moment, pulling the headphones from his ears. He might have missed exactly what she said, but he seemed to intuit the final question.

He threw a bracing glance at the tiles, then swung himself down to the grass.

"It *should* be all right," he said tentatively. "According to my...my experience, these kinds of things tend to dry within forty-eight hours. I don't see it raining until then."

There was a subtle pause. He lifted a hand to the sky.

"Not that I checked, it's just...it's sunny."

Molly spilled her hair forward, trying to hide her grin.

Clairvoyant hilarity aside, she knew for a fact that Julian didn't have any idea in hell what he was doing. His 'experience,' as he so casually described it, was no doubt the hasty call he'd made to Devon the second they were out of sight. His friend might have little more experience with roofing, but he had access to the internet. No doubt he'd talked him through each step, until it was finished.

"That's excellent," Eleanor crooned, smoothing his shirt, "very well done. Thank you so much, sweetheart. I hope it wasn't too much of...*oh my*—whatever happened here?!"

She inched down the top of his shirt and poked a manicured finger at the crescent-shaped scar at the base of his neck. There was one that Molly was familiar with, but the one her mother had spotted was relatively new—courtesy of a human-trafficker who'd bitten him a few weeks before.

"Oh, uh..." He glanced down, pausing ever so slightly. "Cat bite."

You could say that. The man shifted into a panther.

"You should have used one of those water pistols," Eleanor said knowingly, "or maybe some pheromones. They bottle them now, you know? Works wonders in terms of soothing cats."

He stared a moment, then nodded with a faint smile. "I honestly didn't think of that."

Molly snorted with laughter, clapping him on the arm as they headed inside. He had supplies to put away and they had groceries to unload. They also had certain boundaries to discuss.

"Great job, Mom." Molly joined her in the kitchen. "Way to get *real* close."

Eleanor glanced up with false surprise. "You're imagining—"

"You're intruding," Molly corrected, shaking her head with a grin. "Like *way* intruding."

At that point, her mother turned around and looked at her like she was being very slow, planting one hand on her hip, as the other gestured openly out the window.

"*Look* at that boy, Molly. Why on God's green earth didn't you marry him instead?"

Molly threw up her hands, unable to hold back her laughter. "Because I fell in love with *Luke*, Mom. You know—Luke? The father of my child? The one who looks like the reincarnation of Zeus?" When that failed to make an impact, she gestured again to Julian. "I can't believe you're making me say this, but he's got a wife."

Her mother scoffed, as if such things were easily dealt with.

"Oh, it's like that?" Molly scrolled through her gallery for a moment before holding up a picture on her phone. "*This* is his wife."

There was a reluctant pause, then Eleanor paced carelessly to the stove.

"She's blonde."

"*Excuse* me?" Molly laughed again, unable to reconcile the sound. She leaned against the counter as her mother began cutting vegetables, arms folded across her chest. "What's wrong with being blonde? Marilyn was blonde. What if I had been born blonde?"

"We would have dyed your hair immediately," her mother replied without pause. "The hospital was next to a beauty salon. We could have done it right there in the sink."

At this point, Molly honestly didn't know whether she was joking. *Probably not.*

"Stop judging me for judging *other* people," her mother demanded, pulling out a cutting board and a large knife. "Whose side are you on, Molly? This used to be fun."

Molly's eyes lingered on the blade, then she stepped closer.

"It *is* fun," she answered lightly, taking one for herself. "I just think we might want to start with someone different than Angel. Her hobbies aren't quite so harmless as the rest of ours."

Eleanor flashed a quick look, positioning a tomato on the chopping block. "Why? What does she do?"

Molly twirled the knife, then gave it a sudden swing. "She makes bombs."

THAT NIGHT'S DINNER was one of the happiest that Molly could remember.

They cooked it together. Walking around barefoot in the kitchen, sharing random bouts of laughter over an open bottle of wine. It was a level of relaxation that Molly could never have imagined, one that had always seemed to vanish with the oxygen when her mother walked into a room. The wine had been Julian's idea, and it eased them in. The music had been Molly's, and it wasn't long before the usual scripts and deflections were forgotten, lost in the magic of the night.

They'd been tasked with making some pasta dish that Molly would never remember. She and Julian were rubbish, but her mother supervised every moment with a critical eye. Strangely enough, when it became clear there was no point in shaming them, the conversation loosened still further, lapping over them in little waves as the sun dipped lower in the sky.

"So, explain something to me," Eleanor began, fingers wrapped around her glass, "it's been almost twelve hours since you arrived...and you've yet to even mention your precious daughter."

Julian lifted his head, flushed and smiling. "I'm sorry," he said with a mock frown. "Are you asking to see a picture? Maybe ten pictures? Shall we start it from there?" A phone emerged from his pocket and he scrolled briefly through his gallery, selecting one with a tender expression and holding it proudly in view.

Eleanor tilted the screen, a hand cupped over her mouth. "Oh, my goodness...she's exquisite."

And blonde.

Julian nodded in blissful agreement, flipping through a few more. "She's a dream," he murmured, eyes dancing with the glow. "There's one of her by the easel, she did those etchings herself. And that's one of her with our dog..."

Eleanor flashed him a quick look, obviously debating his use of the word 'dog.' The Decker family had grown oddly blind to the fact that a literal wolf slept amongst them. The only time they saw it now was in the flashes of fear and surprise on other people's faces. She was about to say as much, when her eyes fell suddenly upon the tiny design, shimmering in the crook of his arm.

"Heavens me—what in the world is this?"

She reached without thinking, taking hold of his wrist.

"Oh, darling, you have such lovely skin. Why would you go and..." She froze with a sudden jolt of understanding, catching the flush of his cheeks. There was a split second where none of them dared to move, then she released him just as fast. "Right...of course. My apologies."

In the space of a heartbeat, all the momentum they'd been building abruptly stalled in heavy silence. It weighted their tongues and stole all sense of balance—souring the taste of wine in their mouths. It was the kind of moment that Molly had been dreading. The kind she'd been expecting.

The kind that might have derailed the entire evening, but as it turned out, it did something much worse than that. Because her mother didn't *want* to derail the evening.

So she attempted to find a middle ground.

"Right, well, that's just..." Her eyes searched the tablecloth for answers. "It's nothing that we can't..." She faltered a moment longer, then pushed abruptly from her chair. "Just wait a moment."

She vanished from the kitchen, as the friends stared after her in shock—palms pressed to the edge of the table, like they were just a few seconds from leaving themselves. For the life of her, Molly had no idea what in the world might be happening upstairs. Julian's eyes clouded tentatively into the future, but he seemed too afraid to check. Perhaps it would have been better if he had.

It would have given them some time to prepare.

"Mom?" she called tentatively.

A voice echoed down the stairs. "Just a moment!"

The clock ticked on the wall between them, counting off each excruciating breath. They ignored it as best they could, but they were children in that house. Not agents.

"I'm sorry," Julian murmured, tugging guiltily at the cuff of his sleeve. "We're so used to it back in London, I didn't even think—"

"Don't apologize," Molly cut him off quickly. "You didn't do anything wrong. And maybe this isn't..." She trailed off, chewing nervously on her lip. "I thought things were going really well."

He took her hand beneath the table just as her mother sailed down the stairs.

The shock had vanished—kept at bay by a bottle of pills she kept in her purse. The dismay had vanished also, replaced with a look of steely determination as she swept across the kitchen with something clasped tight in her hand. By the time Molly realized what it was, she was already offering it across the table—gesturing with a quick finger to the ink on his arm.

"On you go, love. Out of sight, out of mind."

He reached for it slowly, not immediately understanding. "A bandage?"

Molly was at a similar loss.

Her mother was usually so subtle about threats—working them into her opponents like a splinter beneath the nail. Outright violence wasn't usually her style.

"What are you...?" Her mouth fell open, as it suddenly clicked. "You *can't* be serious."

"It's fine," Julian said swiftly, understanding at the same time. He ripped it open without a second's pause, taping it over his tatù with a tight smile. "It's *fine*."

The second one was strictly for her, a warning under his breath. But she couldn't for the life of her understand how things had taken a turn so quickly. What made it worse was the lingering smile on her mother's face. She thought this was progress. She thought this was okay.

"How about me?" Molly asked stiffly. "Don't I get one, too?" She folded her arms, staring at the woman across the table. "It might need to be bigger. Mine takes up most of my lower back."

It didn't, but her mother didn't know that. Her mother had never dared to look.

A grating silence fell over the room, one that heightened every emotion and amplified every breath. For a terrible moment, it held them all in suspension, then Julian pushed to his feet.

"How about a walk?" he suggested bravely, the only one of them to manage a smile. "It's a lovely evening, and we won't want to be indoors when the roof caves in."

The women stared across the table like he hadn't spoken, never tearing their eyes away.

By now, every trace of the happy evening had shattered and disillusionment was settling in hard. Why had they ever thought this was possible? Why had they even tried?

"A walk sounds nice," Molly finally answered. "We can get a little fresh air."

Rip that bandage off your skin.

Julian leaned forward, catching her mother's gaze.

"Eleanor, would you join us?" he coaxed. The psychic had different standards when it came to immovable family problems. The night had been such a huge success thus far, he was determined to salvage what remained. "They say it's good in terms of recovery."

Her lips curved obligingly, but she shook her head. "You kids go on. I think I'll turn in early tonight."

They left the moment their dishes were cleared, picking up their coats in silence and filing out the door. Eleanor pretended to bustle about in the kitchen, even reminding them to stay clear of the culvert as they departed, but she stared out the window as they headed down the cobbled lane.

She continued staring long after they'd vanished into the night.

"CAN YOU BELIEVE THAT?!" Molly exclaimed, throwing her hands to the sky. "I mean, can you even *believe* that?! A bandage for your arm! And on tonight of all nights!"

It wasn't the biggest town to be exploring, there was a good chance they could have trekked along happily and remained undisturbed. But she and Julian had left it far behind, zipping up their jackets and wandering off the cobbled lanes into the open wilds of the Scottish moor.

The first time he'd visited, they'd been almost afraid to leave the protective glow of the streetlamps—though they'd polished off two bottles of wine and ventured out in the end. Neither one of them had the greatest sense of direction, and both of their partners had made them promise never to attempt such a thing again. But there was something irresistible about such a skyline.

And they'd had quite a bit of wine again tonight.

"It's fine." Julian chuckled under his breath, peeling the bandage off his skin and stuffing it into his pocket. "Seriously, Molls. Don't make it into a big deal."

She whirled around where she stood, trampling a brush of heather.

"A big deal," she echoed with a bit of a slur. "It's your freaking *ink*, Julian. You'd punch someone in the face if they told me to cover mine. Out of sight, out of mind..." She shook her head, slipping into a brooding impression. "What's a seven-letter word for a burden one inherits?"

"Alright," he soothed, "let's just calm—"

"It's a-mother!"

He pursed his lips, eyes twinkling against the dark sky. They listened as echoes of the world faded away into the distance before he extended a gentlemanly arm.

"Feel better?"

I do, a little.

They linked their arms together, continuing off into the night.

The sky seemed bigger than the one in London—with more expanse to cover and fewer buildings to punctuate the view. It was also brighter, *much* brighter. With no urban light pollution corrupting the image, Molly was able to make out the outline of each and every star.

She let out a sigh, resting her head against Julian's shoulder. "I really thought we were making progress tonight," she said quietly. "The same way that I did yesterday. We were laughing, making jokes. It was the first time in longer than I can remember that we struck up a genuine conversation, and then...something always gets in the way."

The tatù on her back tingled with a belated chill.

"I think you *were* making progress," he answered gently, glancing down with a sad smile. "I think your mother's always had trouble getting past the cosmetic. But that doesn't change the way she feels about you. She cares, Molls. *Desperately*. And she doesn't feel like she's a part of your life."

Molly stiffened defensively, already prepped with a reply. "And whose fault is that—"

"It's her fault," he said simply, easing things back down. "I know exactly how many times you've tried to reach out of her, I was there half the times you called. But at this point, it's not about whose fault it was. The two of you are entrenched. You need to deal with that part of it first."

Entrenched.

It was a sad state of affairs when the most accurate way of describing a relationship was using the same terminology as when recounting a war.

"Deal with it," Molly muttered caustically, like it was that easy. "Jules, tonight we saw her literally putting a Band-Aid over a bullet-hole. The woman is beyond help. It's impossible."

The psychic pursed his lips, like he didn't entirely agree.

Julian Decker didn't register words like 'impossible' the same as other people. If it wasn't seen as an outright challenge, it was more of a baseline for things yet to come. But in this particular situation, he'd been working against some especially staggering odds.

"I thought my father would never come out of the future," he said quietly. "I thought *that* was impossible. When he finally did, I thought the two of us would never be able to reconcile, never get to know one another. Never be able to make up the time that was lost."

He drew in a breath, feeling the weight of each word.

It was a clean summary for a mess that had been decades in the making. The terrible story of Jacob Decker could be matched only by the echoes of devastation in the life of his son.

"There is no making up for lost time," he finally concluded. "All those years we missed, they're gone forever. There's nothing to be done about it, no matter how hard I try."

She nodded mutely, then shot him a sideways glance. "That's a really uplifting story, Julian."

He let out a breath of laughter. "You're such an arseling. I'm trying to help you—"

"By telling me the damage is already done and it's too late to fix it?" she interrupted, dodging his teasing swipe. "By telling me some sob story that ends, you know—badly?"

He caught her in a headlock, unable to stop his grin. "I'm *trying* to say...stop reaching backwards. Stop trying to recover things that are already gone. You two had a good day. Focus on that. Try to have a good day tomorrow."

Coming from anyone else, it might have been seen as a dismissal. But the man knew what he was talking out. He'd put in the hours, he'd done the work.

She smiled in spite of herself, staring up at him. "Simple as that, huh?"

He gave her a wink. "Simple as that."

They slowed their pace then, and continued walking toward the horizon. There was little chance of running into trouble—though he was sleepy and not relying on his visions, and her aim tended to waver a bit when she was drunk. Short of the mythical monsters that prowled the misty hills, the most that could trouble them were a few rabbits or maybe a confused-looking deer.

It was one of those nights that could have drawn on forever—lifting above the reach of conventions like daybreak and time. The mist seeped into them, dampening their hair and filling their lungs with the scent of thistles and heather. The ground itself seemed to grip them, clinging around their boots with each step and pulling them back toward the earth.

They stopped on the crest of a small hill, gazing back toward the town.

In London, things would still be twinkling. The night never fully claimed that city. No matter how many times they dragged their weary bodies home, they could always see it coming from miles away. But Evanton was dark and quiet as a whisper, notched into the skyline and blessed with sleep.

"You want to hear something strange?" Molly murmured. "I'm wearing her perfume."

He flashed her a quick look. "You are?"

"Yeah, smell."

She lifted her wrist to his face, staring into the distance as he leaned toward it.

"What is that?" he murmured, taking another sniff. "It's like...molasses?"

She shrugged, tilting her head back to the stars. "One of life's great mysteries. I've never been able to figure it out."

They stood there a while longer, hands dug deep into their pockets, leaning against each other without thinking as their bright eyes stared into the night. It took a few minutes to realize that her face was wet. Another minute to register it was because she was crying.

She let out a silent breath, dabbing her cheeks with her sleeve.

"There's just never been any space around her. She's always been a closed unit—no room for anyone else. Even when I was a kid, I had to work so hard to make her smile."

He glanced at the top of her head, eyes shining with a look she would never see. Then he gathered her into his arms, warming away the shivers and pressing a kiss to her hair.

"You never had to do anything to make me smile."

Chapter 9

The evening was easier after that.

The friends wandered back to the house, flipped on the television, and sprawled out on the living room floor. Molly quickly pulled out her wedding magazines, propping up a pair of absurdly-sized slippers, while Julian watched a football match and ate the last of her mother's ice cream.

It was an adolescent regression at its finest. The kind of unburdened relaxation that was becoming harder and harder to achieve once they'd had children of their own.

The supernatural work-schedule didn't help.

"Your mom goes to sleep crazy-early," he remarked, slumping against the pillows while his eyes followed the players on the screen. "Or maybe I'm just used to working on case files until two in the morning." He sank in farther, stretching his long legs. "I'm also in love with this couch."

Molly smiled absentmindedly, flipping through her magazines. "She needs to return to the cave before sunrise, or she turns to stone."

He let out a breath of laughter, tunneling into the chocolate with his spoon.

There were probably a thousand other things he needed to be doing, a thousand other places he needed to be. But no matter how many hours they wiled away, he never seemed pressed for time.

He was there for Molly. He would be there as long as she needed.

"Do you have the Wi-Fi password?" he asked suddenly.

She gave him a pointed look. "She won't give it to me."

He glanced up in surprise to confirm it, then returned to his ice cream with a grin. "Have you tried Abaddon?"

Molly pushed back her hair with a sigh.

"Beelzebub, Gomory...I went through all the higher demons. The identity of her keeper remains unclear." She turned the page, then paused to examine a dress. After a few seconds, she thrust the magazine toward him. "What do you think about this one?"

He shrugged, then pointed to another. "That's pretty."

She slapped down his hand.

He smiled to himself, having been asked his opinion and given such a response many times before. It was a joke he and the others had channeled into Luke's bachelor party. Each of them had brought some fine gift—a bottle of aged whiskey, a couple's weekend to repair the first inevitable fight in Prague. Julian had presented him with an antique sword. He'd brought an ice-pack as well.

"So, how's the wedding planning going?"

It was a question he'd avoided asking thus far. Partly because he could see the future, and partly because in all of human history, it was a question that had never once gone over well.

Sure enough, Molly had some mixed feelings.

"Well, I mean...it's a journey, isn't it? You know the old saying: you're not planning a wedding, you're discovering something new about yourself."

Julian inched his hand to the remote, turning up the volume on the match. "...is that a saying?"

From that point on, there was no stopping her.

She took just a single breath—the kind all her friends had learned to fear—then she proceeded to launch into a one-woman diatribe about the elegance of the ceremony, the inherent dangers of the guest list, and the critical importance of selecting things like glassware early on.

It was hardly necessary for him to be sitting there. Such speeches required no audience, merely the fervent devotion of a slightly warped mind. But she did enjoy stretching her legs across him as she pontificated towards the ceiling, stealing a bite of ice cream from his spoon.

"—which is exactly the kind of thing we successfully avoided with *my* wedding," she concluded proudly. "Did I ever tell you that the resort coordinator called it—"

"—the most spectacular event she had ever seen," Julian finished with a smile. "I think you did tell me that. A couple hundred times."

Because it's true.

Molly leaned back with a little smirk, proudly replaying each moment in her head.

Truth be told, it was a lot smaller than she'd envisioned her wedding as a child. They had been set to rent out a villa in French wine country, Carter had even agreed to loan them the agency jet, when she'd caught Luke at the table one night, staring longingly at pictures of the beach.

A wedding in the tropics. It was something she'd never considered.

One sweet conversation and a few hundred phone calls later, the plan changed. The cheese plates were returned, twelve pounds of caviar were cancelled, and the bridesmaids gleefully went out shopping for bikinis instead. The only problem that she'd really had was the sand.

"It's going to get all in my dress," she'd said to Rae in the moments before. They were standing in the 'preparation tent' with the other bridesmaids, preparing to walk down the aisle. "I don't know why I agreed to a beach. This is *Italian lace*, Rae. It's going to get all covered in sand!"

Rae peeked her head out the flap before pulling it back with a start. "I don't think you need to worry about the sand..."

Molly sucked in a terrified breath and poked her head outside as well. At that point, she'd half-prepared to find either a disastrously-timed sleeper wave, or an army of supernatural separatists come to ruin her big day. But it was nothing like that. The sand on the beach hand vanished, and there was nothing but a blanket of delicate ivory flower petals as far as the eye could see.

She let out a soft gasp, then turned back to Rae. "You did this?"

Her best friend performed miracles on a daily basis. It wasn't hard to believe that she'd pull off something truly spectacular—such things were required of the maid of honor.

But Rae pursed her lips, tilting her head toward Angel.

Molly's jaw fell to the ground. *"You?"*

The girl was lounging beside the champagne tower, draped in a stunning gown of ice-blue silk. She took a second to register the question, then lifted her shoulders in a casual shrug.

"You said you were worried about the sand."

Rae and Molly exchanged a look.

"But how...?" Molly trailed off as the breeze picked up, filling the tent with the delicate scent of roses of sun. "Where did you possibly get that many flowers?"

The music started and Angel hopped off the table—tossing her headphones into a purse, as she prepared to head down the aisle. "I raided a wedding farther up the beach."

The girls regarded her in silence, then turned to look in the same direction.

"On that note, we might want to hurry this along..."

Molly and Julian laughed quietly, both remembering the same thing. He'd been standing on the other end of the aisle, manically checking the future to make sure nothing would go wrong.

"I never found out how she did that," she murmured.

"She broke into a dive shop and approached from the sea."

There was a pause. Then Molly turned with a solemn expression.

"She's a really good friend."

We're going to need more of that initiative for this next one.

There was a beep in the distance, and they peeled themselves off the sofa. Molly went to retrieve the laundry, as Julian began folding it with her on the floor. The fire had started to dwindle, and the match had stretched into overtime. It could have been any of a hundred such nights they'd spent together. This one just happened to be in a witch's house on the crest of a moor.

As usual, the psychic was thinking along the same lines.

"Do you remember the first time we did this?" he asked quietly, glancing over with a little smile. "When we left Rae unattended by the machines, and she set the whole thing on fire?"

Molly stifled a shudder, remembering the rebuke they'd earned from Madame Elpis.

"Melted my Burberry blouse to ribbons. And that was *before* she learned to conjure."

He shook his head thoughtfully, folding a random pair of pants. "I know our world sees her as some kind of savoir for all the good she's done, but honestly, if they could see the other side...?"

They shared a meaningful look, nodding in agreement.

The problem with the famous Kerrigan gang, was that none of them considered themselves to be the most extreme. Luke and Devon would claim to be the most normal, but one was heir to a medieval monastery, and the other bench-pressed his car in his spare time. Molly created accidental electrical storms every time she ran out of coffee, Julian spent half his time patrolling the future, while two of their members were literally raised in a subterranean version of supernatural hell.

But there was that time Rae had melted the laundry...

"She's a menace," Molly said plainly. "And that was before the time she tried to conjure a wendigo for Halloween. I swear that thing actually took a breath." She lifted her eyes as the logs capsized in the fire. "Would you mind grabbing a few more of those? The woodpile's out back."

Julian glanced out the darkened window. "By myself?" he demanded. "After that?"

She stared at him. "Are you serious?"

There was a beat.

"...no."

Armed with nothing more than a crippling sense of male pride, he pushed warily to his feet, slipping his arms into the thick sleeves of his jacket. The pockets were empty, save for a crumpled brochure he'd stolen from the airline and a forgotten stick of gum. Nothing remotely useful.

"This is a mistake," he breathed. "It feels like a mistake."

She tilted back her head with a burst of merry laughter.

"I can't believe you right now—it's like, twenty paces away." She laughed again when he didn't move. "Check the future if you're so worried."

He flashed a sullen glare. "You know animals are unclear."

She sobered immediately, staring up at him with wide eyes. "You think it would register as an animal?" she whispered, shivering dramatically. "I'm not so sure. It walks on two legs, after all. And it has those wraithlike hands—"

"That's it. Do it yourself."

"Oh, come on!" she laughed. "I'm teasing!"

I might not be teasing.

"Nope." He shook his head, dark hair spilling around his eyes. "We've talked about it too much, and now I'm picturing it...I can't go outside by myself. You have to come with me."

She picked up another sweater, grinning ear to ear. "Phone a friend, Jules."

"*You're* my friend."

"Not anymore," she answered flatly. "My friends are brave."

He leveled her with a cold look. "Tell you what, I'll go fetch some wood from the pile, if you go upstairs and check on your mother. The woman just had surgery, Molly. We're supposedly here to help."

She went still as a grave. "I'll get the wood. You check on my mother."

"Don't be ridiculous," he said loftily, feeling a good deal better about himself now that she was suffering too. "She's already in her bed, Molly Elizabeth. Have you no sense of shame?"

...not really.

"Fine," Molly snapped, pushing to her feet as well. "And I can tell you think this is a real win for you, but Julian, I have absolutely no problem checking on my mother. I'm impervious to her tricks by now. She can't sneak her way inside my head."

He nodded slowly, watching as she inched toward the stairs. It was a comically long journey, but she'd almost made it to the banister when she called suddenly over her shoulder.

"Jules—"

"You don't have an androgynous voice."

Just making sure.

MOLLY TRUDGED SLOWLY up the stairs, dragging her feet to such an extent it was a miracle she didn't scuff the wood beneath them. Despite her false claims of bravery, she was highly aware that Julian had gotten the better deal—wendigo or not. The only thing that kept her going was imagining the look on his face if she were to chicken out and return to the living room. That and the pictures.

She *loved* the pictures.

It was one of the things her family had always done well—documenting the whimsical corners of their lives and mounting them proudly on every available inch of wall. There were framed portraits and photo booth pranks. Even a few pieces of childhood artwork had survived the move.

She paused in front of a well-loved favorite, touching her fingers to the glass.

At a glance, most people would have assumed it was a picture of her as a baby, but they would have been wrong. When she was little more than a toddler, she had lost a sister.

Isabelle.

Few people knew that. She'd only ever told Rae. Not even Luke knew about it until after they were married. It was one of the reasons she was so scared during her pregnancy. Isabelle had been premature and gotten sick, her body never got over it. She'd died less than a year later.

It was only of the few pictures they'd gotten to take.

She walked a few steps further, trailing her fingers along the wall, then paused at another. It was another favorite, though she was surprised to see it mounted with the rest. She was wearing a bright red coat and heading to Paris a week before her sixteenth birthday.

A week before a new world opened, and her old world fell apart.

She remembered the night her father had told her—when he'd rolled up his sleeve and she'd first heard the word tatù. She'd reacted pretty much the same as any child being introduced to the world of magic. She didn't believe him. She was worried for him. She wet the corner of a washcloth and attempted to wipe the offending marker from his arm.

Then he fired off a burst of sparks, and she'd fainted on the hotel room floor.

Of course, her mother wouldn't find out until years later. That was the way it was back then, before Carter ascended to the presidency and changed the rules. Generally speaking, it was a happy time in the magical community. A feeling of profound relief as that heavy weight finally gave free.

Not so much in my house.

That was the day it had ended. That was the day all those pictures had come down.

It was bad enough when she found out about the tatù. In a twisting of the knife, she had the same impulse as her daughter and tried frantically scrubbing it off her skin. But strangely enough, it was the school that bothered her more. Not only was her daughter a freak of nature, marked for life, but she would be separated because of it—different friends, different university, different job.

It was all the *different* that proved to be too much.

In the years that followed, Molly had blocked out most of the aftermath, but there were still parts she remembered—echoes of her mother's frightening, all-consuming rage. There had been shouting, lots of shouting. At one point, a wine glass had shattered against the wall.

And then...nothing.

She paused outside her parents' bedroom door, reaching for the handle before her arm lowered slowly to her side. It wasn't worth it. She could endure Julian's laughter, accept the hug he'd surely give afterward, then the two of them could get on with their night.

Or you could be a good daughter and check on your mom.

With a little sigh, she tip-toed into the room. There was a lump in the center of the bed.

"Mom...are you awake?"

Silence.

She ghosted across the room, measuring her steps the same way she did on a mission. It felt suddenly much harder to be in that room than any of the dangerous things she'd done in the weeks and months before. She would have traded anything to be on a Malaysian freighter, or sneaking into the security vault of a Venetian bank. *Anything* except standing beside her mother's bed.

There was a checklist for medication, and the box for that evening had been left blank. She rummaged quietly in the nightstand, hoping to find the correct bottle and simply leave a note on top for the morning. But her hands froze in the air, as she stumbled upon something different instead.

This can't be...

All the memories she'd been missing, all the pictures that had been taken down from their places in the hall—they were all there. Crammed into that little drawer. Safely out of sight, yet right where her mother could reach them. The edges of most of them had been worn smooth with the fretting of anxious fingers, holding them beneath the lamp light, after night, after night.

There were too many to count. So many, they blurred before Molly's eyes.

She and Luke holding hands on the beach at sunset. Two beaming smiles as she and Rae embraced on the sidewalk in front of their new penthouse. The day she'd come home the first semester at Guilder—the flush of excitement on her cheeks when she stepped off the plane.

Some of them were formal—ones that Molly had sent over herself. The family at Christmas, wedding portraits, Benji's first day at school. Others were more candid, even slightly out of focus, as if they'd been taken with the discreet swipe of a phone. They filled up the entire drawer.

And there wasn't a single one that didn't include her face.

A tender smile warmed her face, one that broke through the inherent sadness. She stared a second longer, then left the drawer carefully as she'd found it. The bottle was placed front and center, a note was scribbled across the top. Then at long last, she turned her eyes to her mother.

The woman was nestled in the shadows, tucked so far beneath the blankets, she'd almost vanished completely from sight. Molly stared a moment, then pressed a kiss to her forehead.

"Goodnight, Mom."

Chapter 10

Molly and Julian fell asleep on the couch together, curled up beneath the same blanket with legs spilling over the side. When the sun peeked through the curtains the next morning, they awoke stiff, and hungover, and abruptly sick to death of Scotland.

"The wine was a mistake," Julian groaned, running a hand over his face. "The wine is always a mistake. Why do we never remember that in time?"

Because we live with no consequences. Because we have a friend who can magically heal.

"It wasn't the wine," Molly corrected, forcing herself upright, "it was all that ice cream you stole, you little thief. This is karma you're feeling. Not the wine."

He shoved her onto the floor. "Oh yeah? Because you didn't have any ice cream. And you look terrible."

She reached up and grabbed onto his ankle, but wasn't strong enough to pull him down with her. After a few seconds of trying, she gave up and slumped back against the sofa instead.

"I look glorious."

I want to die.

"Well, aren't you two a sight to behold." Eleanor swept down the stairs and into the kitchen, looking them over with a twinkle in her eyes. "It looks like someone got into a little too much fun."

The matriarch of the Skye family, she had pioneered the concepts of passive-aggressive compartmentalization and a strong reset at the end of each day. Slights and awkward moments were carefully catalogued, but buried with everything else. It was a skill she had passed on to her daughter.

Molly lifted her eyes but couldn't quite get her into focus. "Julian stole all your ice cream."

"That's a lie," he countered immediately. "It was Molly."

She rotated slowly to face him, but her mother only chuckled.

"We can get more ice cream. In the meantime, I'm going to the diner to meet some friends for breakfast. I'd ask you to come, but you weren't invited. And quite frankly, it looks like you've both been living in a bunker underneath the house. Perhaps you'd like to shower and start anew?"

They shared a quick look, then mumbled unintelligibly.

"Excellent." She clapped her hands loudly, smiling again as they both winced. "In that case, I'll see you in a few hours, darlings. Don't get into too much mischief when I'm away."

She was out the door a second later, slamming it cheerfully as she went.

Molly closed her eyes with a grimace, feeling the sluggish pounding of her pulse behind her eyes. She lifted a trembling hand, then armed herself with a single thought.

Coffee. I've got to make some coffee.

She hobbled toward the kitchen, as Julian locked himself in the shower—silently marveling at the number of products and secretly trying quite a few. A strange floral medley followed after him back down the hallway, but neither of them addressed it. They merely sat down at the table and did the same thing as every other spy when they found themselves with a morning of free time.

They pulled out old case reports.

"It's a good thing you didn't check any of these with the rest of your luggage," Julian murmured, scanning through a document detailing how he and Devon scaled a hundred-foot security fence before unintentionally sinking the owner's yacht. "If you had, the good people of Cambodia might be having some very strange conversations right now."

"I never check them," Molly answered, glancing through her field notes, "not even when I'm with Rae. I think Carter would probably have a meltdown if he knew we carried them at all."

The friends lifted their heads, speaking at the same time.

"Secure location."

They'd heard the fateful words more times than they could count—endlessly chided for an apparent disregard for the rules and limitations that kept those things secret. The files themselves were never supposed to leave the PC tunnels—it was a privilege they'd been allowed to take them off campus at all. But it was a privilege that most all the agents shared. Especially the ones who'd had children. There simply weren't enough hours in the day to complete them otherwise.

They tried not to flaunt it and kept those little disobediences to a minimum whenever they could. But none of them would ever forget the day that Devon himself—in a state of sleepless delirium following the birth of his son—had actually pulled out a tactical summary during a visit with the grandparents and started annotating it right there on Carter's front lawn.

"You know Dev still has a scar on his back from where Carter bludgeoned him with the waffle iron?" Julian remarked. "Almost two years ago, the thing still won't fade."

Molly snorted with laughter, taking a gulp of her coffee. "Why doesn't Rae just heal him?"

"She thinks it's sweet," he answered with an evil grin. "She says it's *family bonding.*"

Molly looked up slowly. "You know the really sad part? With her background? She actually thinks that's true."

They worked in silence for a while, passing a pair of pens and highlighters between them, while the coffee pot slowly lowered to empty and Julian got up to brew more. When they'd first started working for the agency, they would have been stressed beyond the brink if more than a few had piled up at a single time, but they'd slipped into a begrudging rhythm about case reports. It wasn't that they were difficult, one simply recounted things that had happened. There was specific language to use, an agency shorthand, but during their initial training, that had been given its own class.

"Do you ever find yourself tempted to write little notes in the margins?" Molly asked with sudden mischief. The hangover was fading and the caffeine was taking hold. "Sarcastic commentary to troll the case manager or maybe just add in just *one* random detail that wasn't actually there?"

She had done this on several occasions. When describing an ambush in the middle of the Sahara Desert, she had once claimed that she and Rae made their escape by boat.

Julian shook his head with a grin. "You forget, I can actually see what will happen if I do shit like that. And one way or another, all these things eventually end up on Cliff Barnes' desk."

He added the last part without thinking, and the two shared a swift look.

The problem with Barnes was the lack of progression—he wasn't openly escalating like the dissidents they were used to, he simply wasn't going away. The people who'd rallied behind him had done so only in conversation; they were still active agents like everyone else. The man himself still sat behind the same desk where he'd worked since the beginning, using words, not weapons, to argue his point. Pretending he didn't know that words *were* weapons of the best sort.

"Is it true he actually showed up at your house after Budapest?" she asked softly, flashing him a quick look. "Dev told me—I've never seen him so pissed off."

As a rule, they didn't talk much about the psychic's time spend in Budapest. It was a mission that had been intended to heal old wounds, but one that had ended up cutting twice as deep. He hadn't been the same afterward. Not for a long time. A few days later, he'd quit the agency.

Julian stiffened, then nodded briskly. "It was really weird, really fast. We didn't even talk much," he admitted. "After I spoke against him at the meeting, I think he just wanted to make sure that I'd actually retired."

Molly stifled a smile and held her tongue.

Julian Decker's 'retirement' had become a longstanding joke around the Privy Council. It had lasted all of about five hours, then he was back in Carter's office, begging to be reinstated.

"He must have been pretty disappointed," she said lightly.

"Must have been."

They sat there a few minutes longer, rifling through piles of papers and frowning at things they were supposed to read, before she flung down her pen.

"I can't do this anymore. It's been three hours. My hand is falling off."

"Toughen up, Skye," he replied, stretching out his arms. "There's plenty more to go."

He reached into her bag and pulled out another handful of files, including the stack of paperwork she'd been avoiding. She'd brought it with her on the plane, just to make herself feel proactive, but in the time that she'd spent in Scotland, it had yet to leave her bag.

Julian passed her the folders, then glanced at the papers with a frown. "Why didn't you turn this in? Carter wanted them all two weeks ago."

It was an update of the same forms that every intelligence operative filled out upon entering the agency, the grim logistics and insurance policies that plagued each one. This particular document was the PC's version of a company will. Luke was her proxy and next of kin—everyone knew that already, but they needed to have it on file all the same.

Otherwise I'll take your stuff. That was the way Julian had explained it to her in the beginning. He was still staring at her, waiting for a reply.

"Yeah, I know, I just...haven't gotten around to it yet."

She spoke lightly, but the psychic continued to frown.

"You filled out the entire thing. What's the problem?"

He scanned through the pages, then saw that she hadn't filled out the entire thing. She hadn't filled out her name. He lifted his eyes slowly, tapping the empty line.

"Molly...do we have a *bigger* problem?"

She rolled her eyes and snatched it out of his hand.

The first impulse was to deny it. The second impulse was to smack him for prying. She usually listened to those impulses. But the two had walked the moors in Scotland. He'd folded laundry and peeled potatoes for dinner. She'd fallen asleep last night holding his hand.

"I don't know what to write," she said quietly. "This is the first, I mean...it's the first *legal* thing we've had like that since getting married, and it feels like...it feels like whatever I put down, that's how they'll close the book on me. I don't know what I want it to say—Fodder or Skye."

Julian leaned back slowly, staring at her in surprise.

Most of the trials they faced were universal, the same across the board. But he'd never been faced with that particular question himself. He started to answer, but found himself without a script.

"Does it ever bother you that Angel still goes by Cross when she's working?" she asked nervously, having wanted to ask for a long time. "That it's how she's known around the agency?"

He shook his head without hesitation. "She worked hard to make a reputation for herself. She should get to enjoy it. And I'm not complaining when her enemies think twice upon hearing the name." He tilted his head, catching her troubled eyes. "I'm sure Luke feels the same way. Molly Skye is a bloody badass. Molly Fodder is an incredible wife.

They're both the same person. What does it matter what you put on some form?"

Her cheeks warmed with a blush, and she lowered her eyes to the table. It was exactly what she'd been hoping he'd say, the same answer she'd been grappling with herself. But somehow, it didn't feel like just a form. It felt like a lasting judgement she was rendering on her entire life.

"It doesn't," she said quickly. "It doesn't matter."

Or maybe it's the only thing that does.

THE FRIENDS SEPARATED off not long after.

Julian ventured into the mist with some pencils and a sketchpad, while Molly took a much longer shower herself—the kind that depleted the water heater and made her dream of a Jacuzzi.

She was still toweling off when a door opened and her mother's voice echoed up the stairs.

"Kids? Are you still here?"

"Just a minute," she called back down.

With a speed that only that particular woman could ever inspire, she slipped on a pair of leggings and blouse they'd gotten from the boutique the other day, braided her hair in a quick tumble down her back, then hurried down the stairs—taking them four at a time.

Eleanor glanced up as she breezed into the room. "Ah—you look grungy. I thought you were going to straighten up." She heaved a bag onto the counter, unloading pieces of fresh produce. "This is for dinner, but I thought we might all sit down for a light lunch. You kids have been working the day away."

"No cane?"

"I'm feeling better." Her eyes strayed to the papers strewn across the table.

"Where's Julian?"

Molly flushed self-consciously, dabbing at her braid. "He wanted to sketch the ruins."

"Bit of a dreamer that one, isn't he?" Eleanor whipped out a knife to begin cutting the vegetables. "But it's always nice when someone appreciates the finer things in life."

"The finer things." Molly lifted her eyebrows delicately, knowing firsthand that wasn't usually what her mother had in mind. "A bunch of crumbling rocks and grass."

The knife pointed in her direction. "We are living amidst *pristine beauty*, Molly Elizabeth. At least, that's what all the national guidebooks call it. Don't pass judgement on things you don't understand."

...seriously?

...this is coming from you?

Deciding not to engage, Molly wandered to the table, slowly piecing together the piles they had scattered and sliding them back into her bag. Her mother pretended not to be watching, but her sharp eyes followed every move—straining from afar to read the text.

After a few seconds, she gestured with a careless hand.

"What's all that?"

Molly glanced up swiftly, then continued packing the bag. "It's nothing. Just work stuff."

"Like what?"

Like you care.

"Like...*work* stuff, Mom. For my job."

Eleanor set down the knife, wiping her hands on a towel. "Oh—for your job?" she quipped. "That's what you meant by work?" She flashed a wry smile, then glanced back at the table. "...is that a will?"

Molly set down the bag in exasperation. *"Bloody hell."*

"Language," Eleanor chided, turning back to the carrots with seeming indifference. "You need a will with the kind of work you do. It would be irresponsible not to have one. Your father and I both have one, and he spends half his life sitting on that couch." There was a slight pause with the carrots. "I'm assuming you've already arranged care for Benji? If anything should happen?"

An unsettling thing to say whilst holding a knife.

Molly stared a moment, wondering at the innocent phrasing of the question, the way it seemed almost rehearsed. Then she shoved the last of the papers into her bag.

"He'd stay with Julian. That's his godfather."

There was no point in elaborating any further. No point in revealing Rae's additional claim to him as godmother. No point in listing each of the people in her friend circle—how they would have instant prominence—or explaining that if a bomb should happen to fall upon the little cul-de-sac, the child had an entire community of people that would fight for the position themselves.

There was no point saying any of it, because her mother hadn't made the list.

That being said, mothers had a keen sense for that sort of thing, and there was a good chance Eleanor had intuited as much herself. There was a faint tightening of the eyes around the corners. Her shoulders went suddenly still, as if she was no longer taking a breath.

"So how's your husband getting on?" she asked abruptly. "Is he still teaching?"

Molly blinked in surprise, trying to keep up. "Of course he's still teaching. He just got started." She should have stopped there, but she pushed on a little farther. "Why would you ask me that?"

"Well, you never know, do you?" her mother replied innocently. "It seems he's had so many jobs. First, he was with one agency, then the other. In the tech room, in the field. Now suddenly he wants to play teacher." She popped a cracker into her mouth with a hard smile. "He's a man of many talents. You should appreciate that, darling. He sounds a lot like you."

Molly nodded slowly, never breaking her gaze. "How's your leg?"

They stared at each other a brief moment, then Eleanor set down the knife.

"I'm going to pick up more wine for dinner. You two clearly have a taste for it, and I figured since you're here, we'll give this family bonding thing another go. You don't mind, do you?" She picked up her purse and swept toward the door. "We're having rabbit."

It slammed behind her, and Molly shut her eyes.

"I hate the Highlands," she muttered aloud. "Have some whiskey, tip a cow."

It was unfortunate that Julian walked inside that very moment. He froze abruptly still upon entering, studying her face with concern. "Seriously, hon—how much are you sleeping?"

She dropped into a chair, rubbing her temples. "Sorry, she's just getting down on Luke."

And me. And probably even you, for being a 'dreamer.'

"Luke?" he repeated, settling down beside her. "I thought the two of them were on pretty good terms. He texts her pictures of Benji. How could anyone not like Luke?"

Molly shrugged, face pressed into her hands. "She's found a way."

He rubbed her back, staring into space. "My dad had some trouble with the idea of Angel in the beginning," he admitted. "Before he learned the whole story and got to know who she was. Of course, he wasn't around that much in the beginning, and he doesn't really have a leg to stand on..."

"It's not the same," she sighed. "You married a psychopath, Julian. Now everyone's worried about you. Luke is actually a good man. There's no reason in the world not to like him."

Julian opened his mouth, then closed it deliberately shut. "Let her vent it out," he murmured to himself, ignoring the girl by his side. "This is about her damage, not yours." He felt the need to add, "You knew she was awful before you came here."

She lifted her head from the table.

"Feel better?" she asked sarcastically.

"Feel nicer?" he fired back.

She flashed a pearly smile. "Let's see..."

Without another word, she pushed abruptly from the table—grabbing his wrist and pulling him toward the back door. There was a yard out there somewhere, behind the flowering trellises of her mother's garden. There was a chance her father had even remembered to cut the grass.

"Let's spar."

He pulled back immediately, yanking free his sleeve. "No, you just want to shock me because I liked that dress with the sapphire thing."

"That *dress* was the most depressingly simplistic thing I'd ever seen," she said patiently. "The only reason you liked it, was because that color makes you want to paint."

He opened his mouth, then closed it with a look of surprise. "That's absolutely true."

"No powers, alright? I won't shock you—I promise." She casually reclaimed his arm, tugging him coaxingly toward the door. "Can we just spar for a bit? Get out a little energy?"

I really want to hit something

"SON OF A B—!"

Julian spat and cursed loudly as he hit the ground, somersaulting uncontrollably, before crashing to a stop in what looked unfortunately like a thicket of brambles. His jacket was still smoking from where it had recently absorbed a dangerous amount of electricity, and while he was trying to push himself back up, the muscles in his arms kept twitching from short-circuits in the brain.

"You promised—you unlovable monster," he panted quietly, pressing his forehead to the ground. "You promised you wouldn't use any powers."

Molly stood a few paces away by the jasmine, fingers twisting guiltily behind her back. "It just slipped out—I'm sorry!"

He stopped twitching long enough to give her a cold glare. "*Five times?*"

Six, actually. But I'm pretty sure he blacked out for that last one.

"It's muscle memory, Jules. It's nearly impossible to control." She watched him push shakily to his feet, preparing to level another bolt if he decided to take it personally. "And don't act like you haven't done it yourself. I totally saw your eyes flash that time by the fountain."

"I was checking to make sure you weren't going to blast me *into* the fountain," he countered furiously. "I was checking to make sure I wasn't going to get electrocuted. *Again.*"

She nodded slowly, sensing a bit of hostility. "Not another bolt. I promise."

He paced forward, reaching into his pocket. "You'll do more than that. You'll wear this."

She froze in astonishment as he draped it over her neck. "You carry an inhibitor with you?"

"It never hurts to be prepared," he answered, pressing the button. "You never know where the night might take you. Better safe than sorry."

Why do I feel like I've heard that somewhere?

"What about you?" she complained, chafing against the strange numbing sensation where all that glorious voltage should have been. "Do you have another for yourself?"

Over the last few weeks, the friends had been trying to use their tatù in spite of the presence of an inhibitor. None of them were sure it was even possible, but Carter declared it could only make the ink stronger to try. She always hated those days. She made up any excuse to miss them.

"I have a modicum of self-control," he answered loftily. "Unlike some electric savages I'm cursed to know. Come on then, hotshot. Let's see how your luck holds now."

At that point, Molly began scheming ways to discreetly end their session. She'd been trained by the best Guilder had to offer, but she could never beat Julian in a fight.

That being said, it was incredibly fun to try.

"LET GO OF ME!"

Molly let out a shriek of laughter, pounding desperately at Julian's legs. It was the only place she could reach, given that she'd been placed in an inescapable headlock. While she'd tried a wide array of kicking, biting, pleading, and threatening—there was *nothing* she could do to get free. "Jules, I'm serious! Let me go!"

He leaned calmly forward, making sure to tangle her hair. "*No.*"

He spoke directly into her ear, taking a great deal of satisfaction in every word. Maybe if she hadn't used his body to capsize a birdbath. Maybe if she hadn't criticized his wife.

She bowed her head, shaking with silent laughter.

"Okay...what would *you* do in this situation?"

It was a strategy that she and Rae had used many times to get out of similar conundrums in the past. Their men might be merciless, but they loved the process and they loved to share. Devon in particular was a total sucker for instruction. If his wife was curious how to free herself from his evil clutches and throw him into the adjacent wall, he couldn't help but tell her exactly how.

Julian wasn't quite so gullible. "I'd kill myself."

She snorted with laughter, slamming her head back into his chest. "Come on, enough already! I'm sorry about the fountain!"

His arm flexed ever so slightly, tightening across her throat. "It's just so much nicer when you're quiet," he mused, tilting back his head to gaze up at the darkening sky. "Sometimes, I wonder what it would be like if you were always this quiet. If someone took the initiative to end this little freak show once and for all."

I'm going to shock you so fucking hard.

She stretched her tongue as far as possible, hoping to catch hold of the inhibitor.

"Molly, don't be a child. If you're hungry, just say so."

She thrashed around violently a few more seconds, then hung her head in defeat, going abruptly limp in his arms. His arm vanished immediately, and she dropped into an unceremonious little pile on the grass. When she tried to remove the inhibitor, he slapped down her hand. When she patted the grass beside her, he sat down with a friendly smile.

"Thanks for suggesting that. I feel a lot better."

She leaned against him, stretching out her legs in the grass. "...me too."

They sat there for a while, heads tilted together, as the sun drifted down and kissed the horizon, sending blazing streaks of color across the sky. There was a kind of triumph about it in a way that felt like it should have been louder. But there wasn't a single whisper to disrupt the quiet.

"I'm sorry about all this," Molly murmured, tracing the lines of his palm as they gazed into the sky. "I never wanted to drag you out here. I never wanted to come it the first place."

He smiled absentmindedly, resting his cheek on her hair. "I'm glad you did. These are growing pains, Molls. You just need to break through."

She nodded faintly, playing the last few days in her mind.

There were parts that showed signs of progress, that much was true enough. But every time they reached a certain point, all those old triggers sprang up again and whatever they were starting seemed doomed to fail. Sometimes she wondered if it was inevitable. Sometimes she wondered if they'd be in the exact same situation if that magical ink had never appeared on her skin.

"She said I was a winter, not a spring."

The poet in him came alive, and his mouth fell open in dismay.

"That's a *terrible* thing to say to someone."

She rolled her eyes. "It's a color pallet, Jules. She was talking about clothes."

There was a pause.

"I really don't understand you, sometimes."

She patted his hand and they leaned together once more. "I know."

Chapter 11

Eleanor arrived home when the sun went down, and the three of them proceeded to make dinner in silence. There was a little forced conversation—mostly prompted by Julian. About halfway through, they turned on some background music—also suggested by Julian. But by the time they sat down at the table, the tension pulsing through the room was almost overwhelming.

Three forks scraped against the plates, echoing in the silence.

"So how did your physical therapy end up going?" Julian asked politely, making a gallant effort to break the ice. "I don't think Molly ever told me."

Eleanor flashed him a look, taking a tight sip of water. "They made me walk in a circle, while a twenty-six-year-old with a bovine nose piercing lectured me about the importance of taking care of one's body. It was *brief.*"

He nodded quickly, dropping his eyes back to his plate.

"Did they give you any kind of schedule for that?" Molly asked lightly, pushing things around on her plate without actually eating anything. "I know Dad was worried about—"

"If you're getting restless, there's no need to wait for your father," her mother interrupted sharply. "As you can see from this evening, I'm quite capable of getting by on my own. You have a life to get back to in London. There's no reason for you to stay around here and play nurse."

Julian glanced quickly between them. "I don't think that's what she—"

"I know exactly what she meant. Eat your peas, Julian."

Molly regarded her evenly, arms folded across her chest.

A few years earlier, she might have taken that kind of thing in stride. Another version of herself might have cowered and acquiesced, shaping herself into whatever the demanding woman sitting across the table required her to be. But that girl had vanished when she turned sixteen.

The woman she'd grown into was quite different.

"I'm asking about a schedule because I want to get the logistics copied down. You've been lousy about taking your pills, and I'm worried you'll let things slide if they aren't written on paper."

And YES, I have a life to get back to in London. YES, I want to leave this damned-forsaken town.

Eleanor set her fork slowly on the table, tilting her head like a predatory bird the moment before it decided to strike. "I didn't ask you to come and police me—"

"Of course you didn't," Molly interrupted. "You didn't even tell me that you were having surgery. Why would I think you'd want me here at all?"

The clock ticked loudly on the wall between them.

"Molls, I don't think—"

"Eat your peas, Julian."

The psychic retreated back to his corner, bowing his head and trying very hard to tune out the pair of formidable women sitting at opposite ends of the table. It was a task that would have been significantly easier if he didn't happen to be the only buffer sitting in between.

"Don't snap at your friend," Eleanor chided. "There aren't many people who would fly to the Highlands just to rescue you from your evil mother. You should thank the boy."

"This isn't a rescue, it's a visit." Molly picked up a butter knife, spinning it distractedly between her fingers. "And your words, mother dearest. Not mine."

Julian reached over silently and took the knife away.

"Do you like the roast?" Eleanor asked him with a tight smile, never taking her eyes off her daughter. "It's a strong flavor. Not for everyone."

That's one way of describing it.

"Yeah, it's...I've never had anything like it." He swallowed hard, poking at the rest of it with his fork. "What is it, exactly?"

The woman's eyes glinted in the dim light. "It's rabbit."

He went abruptly still, the fork still balanced in his hands. Her attention was elsewhere, but he kept staring. After a few seconds, he lowered his eyes to the plate, looking like he wanted to cry.

Vintage Eleanor.

"So Julian," she continued briskly, "did this secret council of yours make you complete a will as well? Molly's playing it rather close to the vest, but we aren't even listed as her next of kin."

The psychic froze again, glancing between them.

"We all got those papers," he finally managed. "We get them every few years. Just the agency covering its bases, the whole thing is pretty standard—"

"How do you know who's listed as my next of kin?" Molly asked suddenly, lowering her fork to the table. Her pulse quickened when her mother didn't meet her eyes. "*Mom*, how do you know who's listed? I never told you, and those papers are already in my..."

My bag.

They were certainly supposed to be. She'd tucked them inside herself, just a few hours earlier. Yet there they were, sitting in the middle of the counter.

She turned to her mother slowly, gawking in surprise. "Did you take those out—"

"What was I supposed to do?" Eleanor snapped. "When my only daughter is filling out death insurance on the kitchen counter, I take an interest. I will not apologize for that, Molly."

"An interest?" Molly pushed her chair back from the table, unable to hear anything over the ringing in her ears. "Now suddenly you want to take in interest? Now that I'm gone?"

It was a sharper exchange than either had intended. The entire dinner was shaping up to be the same. But if they'd wanted to stop it, there was an acceleration to such things that was beyond their control. The visit had been a slow-burning disaster. At some point, that tension had to break.

But Eleanor wasn't going to be the one to break it. She might like to peck at it; she might chip away with those perfectly manicured claws. But she held her tongue, staring in perfect silence.

"This is *exactly* what I'm talking about!" Molly continued, throwing up her hands. "When you can't handle something, you just close down and pretend like it isn't happening! You *don't* call, and breeze past like it isn't even there! But the second I decide that *I* no longer wish to share—"

"Glass houses, darling."

Since she was a child, Eleanor Skye had an unsettling way of making people listen when she wanted to speak. She accomplished this not by yelling, but making her voice a dangerous kind of quiet. It was a chilling tactic. One that was just as effective then, as it was now.

"I am not the one who fled Cardiff and decided never to return. I am not the one who abandoned their family the second the opportunity presented itself and decided to become an entirely different person—a person her mother doesn't even know. You talk about a closed circuit; if anything ever happened to you, who would I need to call in order to visit my grandson. *Him?*"

She jabbed a pointed finger toward Julian, but for once, the psychic didn't have some quick answer to diffuse the situation. Quite the contrary, he was looking very much like he'd give anything to exchange that clairvoyance for invisibility, if only for the night.

Molly shoved the plate away, pushing halfway to her feet. "I didn't flee Cardiff, Mom. I went to school. Just like every other kid in the European continent. And forgive me for not returning to Wales like some proverbial wanderer—but you sold my childhood house! You expunged every memory of me that no longer fit into your perfect version of the way things were supposed to be. We went back one time, then it was gone! *You* left, not me!"

Eleanor's eyes sparked, but she didn't back down. She simply leveled her daughter with a chilling expression, like a gust of wind rushing over desiccated leaves. "You were so happy with your life in London, I saw no reason to continue with the house in Wales. Perhaps if you've shown more of an interest—"

"Oh, this is unbelievable," Molly snapped, rising from the table. "You know what? You're right. I should go back to London. You and I do better with thick, international borders in between us. We're no longer at the point where we can share household walls."

Her mother leaned back with a hard smirk, as if she'd expected no different. Whether or not it was what she'd wanted, there was a hollow victory in it all the same.

"If that's the way you feel, I suppose it's for the best. I'll find someone to drive you to the airport in the morning, no need to draw things out. And if it makes you feel any better," she added, as Molly paced toward the door, "you lasted a good two days longer than I thought you would. I'd tell you to keep your distance in the future, but you've never had any problem doing that."

Molly paused in the frame, staring with a fixed expression at the stairs.

Take a breath.

It was a lesson that had taken years to learn and a patience she hadn't possessed when she'd first started trying. It was a lesson learned by hair-raising accident, highlighted in moments of deep remorse, and framed in years of guilt and regret. People did not merely lose their temper when they inherited superpowers. People lost their tempers, and the people around them got hurt.

Badly.

"You think I'm the one keeping their distance?" she asked softly. "You think it's me?"

She turned around slowly, feeling like she was floating an inch above the tiles.

"I called you every single day, Mom. Every single day for a year, and never *once* did you call me back. I'd lie to my friends and say you were supportive, because I was embarrassed to admit any different. I'd duck into the bathroom between classes and check my messages, on the off-chance I'd missed your call. And then you know what I realized? You were never going to call. Because who I was, the person I was growing into...was a person you didn't want to know."

She was shaking now. Shaking so hard, there wasn't any stopping it. A wave of current was building deep inside her body, flying beneath her skin like blood. It lit the backs of her eyes, but she was too beside herself to notice. She was laying herself bare and letting all of those unspoken truths, all of those whispered heartaches she swore she'd never tell, pour out between them onto the floor.

"You say that I left you? That I abandoned my family?" Her eyes flashed and a shower of sparks rained from her hands. "I was piecing myself back together! I was fixing what you broke, Mother. You don't get to be angry that I came out stronger than I was before."

Julian pushed halfway to his feet, poised on the brink of several uncertain futures, but Eleanor was rigid as a statue. Her eyes had followed the sparks, found every little bruise where they'd landed upon the marble. Then they lifted back to her daughter, raw as a split nerve.

"You told me you were *magic*."

The word ripped between her teeth, slicing the air between them.

As long as her daughter had wanted to throw stones, she'd wanted to throw them even longer. She'd ranted in silence, wept furious tears, paced the length of first one house and then another—searching for anything that might help. Anything that might soothe that impossible ache.

Never once did she find it.

"You told me you were magic. You lifted your shirt and showed me the stain. Then you flew off to England and fell into the arms of a hundred people just like you. A hundred people to support you, to help you navigate this impossible new world."

She stood up slowly, straight-backed as her chair.

"Do you know what I did, Molly? After my child told me this great secret? After I found out my husband had been keeping it from me as well? Do you know what I did after I discovered I lived in a world that included magic? A world that had claimed my only surviving child?"

There was a terrible pause.

"I walked back into my house."

She circled around the table, so they were standing face to face. Even then, even with nothing left in between them, they had never felt that distance so sharp as they did that day.

"You drop this bombshell in my lap, then leave me to pick up the pieces. You forget who I am—*who we are to each other*—and come to hate me for not processing it according to your personal schedule, for not taking all those endless phone calls and reassuring you that everything was fine." She shook her head slowly, eyes blazing like a brand. "Well, I'm sorry to disappoint you, darling. But some of us *needed more time*."

Molly stared back in silence, feeling like she was burning from the inside-out. Whenever hurts they shared between them, however many words they used to explain, she had never realized how truly hopeless things were until that moment. The moment she realized that her mother wasn't being cold or distracted or selfish...the woman truly believed that she was right.

"I don't care," she breathed.

There was movement in her periphery, whatever precarious futures Julian had seen, she was hovering right on the edge. He took a step closer, but her eyes were only for her mother. The house had faded into a mere afterthought. What did it matter? She would never be coming back.

"That's your big resentment? That's the reason for all of this?" She gestured to the space between them. "You felt like you weren't given enough space to process? You needed more time?"

The lights flickered, as her voice swelled to a shout.

"I needed more time! ME—your sixteen-year-old daughter! You think *I* was expecting any of this? You think that bombshell didn't get dropped in *my* lap?! I was the one dealing with the disappearance of my identity! All the things that I'd imagined about my life, all my future plans!"

She was rolling now, unable to turn back the clock, unable to even think about stopping.

"My entire world turned upside-down to the point where I still have to think which version of myself I want to write on a piece of paper. And when I looked to my mother...? The one person who was supposed to always show up for me...? You were NOWHERE to be found!"

A flash of lightning split the air, scorching the pristine walls.

"Molly!"

Julian was there a second later, throwing himself between them, as her arms wilted back to her sides. Her mouth was slack and her body was trembling. She couldn't remember the last time she'd done something like that, the last time she'd lost control. Her eyes watered over, spilling in silent streams down her cheeks, but when she pulled in a breath to apologize, it was already over.

The damage was already done.

WHEN JULIAN FOUND MOLLY a few hours later, she was sitting on the roof outside her bedroom window—not far from the broken shingles he'd patched only a day before. He regarded the spot with a hint of concern, eyes flashing toward the future, before climbing out and settling beside her.

"I must not have been clear...but this is *wildly* unstable."

She kept her eyes forward, staring blankly into space. "Is she okay?"

He drew in a breath, then nodded quickly. 'Okay' was a relative word. In this case, neither of the women truly qualified, so it was better to be generous and brief.

"She's up in her room. She took her pills for the evening."

And then some.

Molly shivered again, wrapping her arms around her legs. "I can't believe I did that," she murmured, staring into the burgeoning night. "I thought I was past that point, where it's tied to emotions. Where it can happen beyond my control." She opened her mouth, then closed it again. "You know...that's the first time she's ever seen my ink."

In a way, that was the most painful part of all. So many times she'd imagined how something like that might happen, the look of wonder on her mother's face. It might be reluctant, at least in the beginning. But maybe that could start to change. Maybe it could lighten with a hint of pride.

I killed all chance of that tonight. It must have been her worst nightmare.

He flashed a sideways look, then lowered his eyes to the roof. "You never told me what happened," he said quietly, "after you told her. I know there was a big fight between her and your dad. And I know she stopped speaking to you about it..."

He trailed off, giving her space to finish the rest.

"She stopped speaking to me at all. Four months, not a single word."

It probably should have made more of an impact. It wasn't a thing she spoke of often. But Molly didn't think there was a thing in the world that could rattle her in that moment. The limits had reached and there was nothing left to be impacted. She was just finished. She was just numb.

"Then one day there was a knock at the door," she continued abruptly. "It was the postman dropping off a letter—reminding her to renew a subscription to *Guns & Ammo* magazine." The story stalled, and they locked eyes for a split second. "My mother doesn't have a subscription to *Guns & Ammo* magazine. At least, that was my thinking at the time."

She wiped her cheeks, still feeling the residual voltage in her hands.

"Anyway, I called up to her room, but she obviously didn't answer. So I went upstairs to see her sitting at the vanity, curling her hair..." She trailed off, remembering the moment perfectly. "I told her about the magazine and she just nodded—curtly. She was always curt with me now. But the thing is, she didn't even look at me. Not for a second. Not even in the reflection of the mirror."

A gentle breeze picked up, rippling the grass and washing over them.

"The house was so quiet, Julian. We'd always been talkers, but now it was just...I wanted so badly to laugh about this stupid magazine. I wanted so badly for things to go back to normal, for her to laugh with me and tell me what had gone wrong. But she couldn't even look at me."

She dropped her eyes to her lap.

"And I just...lost it."

The memory darkened then. She was barely able to look at it herself.

"I started screaming at her—loud as I could, anything to make a little noise. It's almost too mortifying to think about now, a full-on tantrum. *Look at me. Just LOOK at me.*"

She shook her head, hearing phantom echoes from the house.

"When she wouldn't do it, I stormed across the room—picked up the curling iron and burned the skin on my arm. She looked at me then, but I wished that she hadn't. She just stared without any expression, then took my wrist between two fingers and held it to the light."

Her lips twisted as she quoted, trying to approximate a smile. "At least *that* one won't scar."

It was the only thing her mother had said. And it was the last time they'd spoken. She'd packed her bags and left the next morning. It was the last time she'd set foot in the old house.

Julian didn't say anything. There was nothing to say. He simply leaned against her, letting her lean back into him. They stayed that way for a long while, watching the slow rise of the moon.

"Did you see that was going to happen?" she asked suddenly. "With the lightning?"

He shook his head. "You didn't decide to do it. I saw...well, I saw things getting pretty heated. But it wasn't anything like that." He hesitated a moment, then flashed a bracing look. "Molly...I also don't think it was the worst thing for her to have seen. No one was hurt, not even the house. That was just *you*."

She turned to him for the first time, tearing her eyes away from the sky.

"People always go on about how smart you are, but Jules, I swear sometimes you aren't even listening. The fact that bolts of lightning shoot from my hands...that's literally her entire problem."

"Exactly, it's *her* problem," he replied simply. "It's nothing that you did wrong, it's not that she hates some fundamental part of you. She's just...limited. To be honest, I don't even think it was done with the worst of intentions. She's right, in her own way. The hurt was real. The shock was real. And your darling mother...isn't the kind of person who can see past something like that. Not on her own. Not without a lot of time. And not without a lot of help. She just isn't capable." He leaned into her farther, giving her a little nudge. "But you are."

She flashed him a quick glance, then rolled her eyes. "I'm the girl who electrocuted her mother's kitchen, while pretending I didn't want to do exactly what she was accusing me of and just leave. I am not some elevated kind of person."

Much to her surprise, his face warmed with a tender smile.

"Of course you are, it's why you're my favorite." He twisted slightly to face her, tucking back a strand of flyaway hair. "Molls, you might want to leave—but you came back here. You hitchhiked across the moor, in a feed cart, just to take care of someone who treats you terribly and makes you want to burn your own skin. You learned her pills and took her to therapy. And while you might fire off occasional bolts of lightning, you took her one great failing and turned it around."

He laced their fingers together, bringing up her knuckles for a kiss.

"You show up for people, Molly Elizabeth. It doesn't matter if the world is actually falling to pieces, you show up. Because you've got the biggest, kindest heart I've ever seen."

She pulled in a shaky breath, eyes spilling over with tears.

"Do you promise?" she whispered. "Because sometimes I feel like a monster."

"You are a monster," he answered without hesitation, "but I know it for sure." There was a slight pause. "The same way I know you're going to go back inside and talk with your mom."

Yeah, that makes sense.

Her head snapped up.

Wait—what?!

"Talk with her?" she repeated in dismay. "But you saw what she—"

He pursed his lips.

"But you heard the things she—"

He pointed a finger at the window.

"Ugh—*fine!*"

She pushed to her feet and stomped toward the house, freezing dead still when two tiles shifted beneath her shoe and clattered to the ground. The two friends sucked in a silent breath, then leaned carefully over the side—gazing down at the shattered bits of plaster.

A few seconds dragged past, then their eyes lifted slowly to each other.

"...I guess it didn't dry?"

She smacked him in the chest. "That could have *killed* me!"

ARMED WITH THE KNOWLEDGE that if everything started to go terribly wrong, she could simply push her best friend off the roof, Molly slipped back through the window and padded down the hall toward her mother's room. The door was shut, as it so often was. She had countless memories of similar such situations as a child—groveling after a fight, bringing favorite things, one after the other, until at some point, she'd return and find the door unlatched and ready for an apology.

It was unlatched already. She took a careful step inside.

"Mom?"

Eleanor was staring blankly out the window, her face a misty reflection in the glass. Unlike those other times, it didn't look as though she'd been expecting company. She hardly glanced up at her daughter's presence now. She merely tightened her sweater, gazing over the moor.

How do I even start? What should I say?

"I'm really sorry about the—"

"You know the first thing I thought when you told me about the tatù? When you told me that's the reason your father had picked Guilder, that it was the whole point of the school?"

Molly froze where she stood, staring in stunned silence.

She didn't know what surprised her most—the fact that her mother was knowingly forgoing an apology, or the fact that she'd used words like *tatù* and *Guilder*. Even after so many years, she truly didn't think they were in her vocabulary. Like she'd found a way to genuinely block them out.

"I wanted to go with you."

...excuse me?

If Molly was stunned before, she was flat-out confounded now. Acting on some strange impulse, she took a step closer—unable to do anything but repeat the words.

"You wanted to come with me?" she repeated incredulously. "Like...to the school?"

Eleanor smiled faintly, still staring out the glass. "Not to the school, per say. But into that world. What are you kids always calling it? The *supernatural community*." She shook her head, clouding the window with every breath. "The first time I heard those words...I can't tell you the images I conjured. Witches on broomsticks, giant wolves and elves. You talked about it all so...so *practically*, like it was just something you'd taken in stride. I didn't understand how you could do that. I was nothing but afraid. But that didn't matter. If you were going, then I wanted to go with you. To protect you. But there wasn't a place for me there."

I must he dreaming. This can't be real.

Molly took a step closer, pressing the door gently shut.

"To protect me," she couldn't help repeating, trying to mask the surprise.

In a flash, she imagined all the people who'd ever come after her, all the ways that beautiful magic had been made twisted and dark. Then her eyes drifted back to her mother.

She could not picture the two together.

Much as she tried to hide it, the sentiment must have come through in her voice, because Eleanor glanced over her shoulder, then let out a humorless laugh.

"It seems funny to you, doesn't it? Of course it does. Why shouldn't it?" The smile lingered, but her voice grew abruptly sad. "What place is there in all that wonder for someone like me?" She turned around then, wiping at her cheeks. "I imagine it was a relief when your father told you," she added quietly. "As if the two of you needed something else to bring you together, something that excluded your tiresome mother."

Molly circled slowly around the bed, face stinging as though she'd been slapped. "You know that's not true," she argued softly, shaking her head. "I only ever wanted you to be a part of it. I only ever wanted to share it with you, Mom."

"And I didn't want to bury another daughter."

Time slowed to a stop, as the pair locked eyes.

If there was a single thing the Skye family talked about less than magic, it was the little girl framed in a picture on the hallway wall. Molly couldn't remember the last time she'd heard her mother address it. She couldn't remember the last time any of them had said her sister's name.

"You know...Izzy was perfect, until she got sick. Not a thing in the world wrong with her. She had enough food and water. Blankets and doctors. In the ten months she was with us, I could count on one hand the number of times she left my side. Then all at once...she was gone."

Eleanor shook her head blankly, like she'd been roused from a heavy sleep.

"I never realized it was so easy," she breathed. "That life was such a fragile thing. One day, she was tucked in her cradle by the window, and the next..." She lifted her eyes slowly, turning from one daughter to the next. "You think I hate the magic? You think I hate the fact that you can do these wondrous and inspiring things? Things that help people? Things that save lives?"

Her eyes spilled over with silent tears and Molly watched, not sure how to answer or if she should.

Eleanor swallowed and shook her head. "People shoot guns at you, sweetheart. You run into burning buildings, you jump out of planes. Half the time, I have no idea what country you're in or whether you're lying in some field hospital, gasping for breath. You're just making it...*so easy* for something to take you away."

She might have said more. Now that the floodgates were open, she might have kept talking for hours. But the two would never know. Because no sooner had she said that last sentence, than Molly closed all the distance between them—embracing her mother in a fierce hug.

"That's *not* going to happen, do you hear me?" she whispered, arms locked around her mother's fiery hair. "If you knew the people I had around me, if you knew the training we've been given. If you knew half the things I can do myself...that's just *not* going to happen."

Never had her mother seemed so fragile as she did in that moment. Her strong, cold, fearless mother. The one who always had the answers, sculpted to perfection, shaking with silent sobs.

"You can't know that," she breathed. "You can't know what the future might hold."

Molly's eyes flew open, then warmed with a secret smile.

"Not to ruin the moment, but we *might* want to have another chat about Julian..."

They held on a few minutes longer, eyes closed and gently swaying, not wanting to be the first one to let go. Then she gave a final squeeze, leaning back with the same watery smile.

There was a soft chorus of laughter, as they wiped mascara from their cheeks.

"You know this is *exactly* what Dad was planning," Molly teased, her pulse still fluttering away in her chest. "At this point, I wouldn't be surprised if he'd actually sabotaged your knee."

"Molly Elizabeth, that is a perfectly vulgar thing to say. At the same time, it's hard to not to see the logic. No matter, we'll have to plan something equally terrible for when he comes home."

The two shared another look, then turned away with matching smiles.

"That's if you're staying that long," her mother added, glancing out the window. "Those vans that have been parked out front. I suppose that's your rescue team?"

Molly glanced up in surprise. "What?"

"More friends to save you from Scotland and bring you back into the magical fold," Eleanor explained, tilting her head toward the window. "I assume that's why they've come?"

They locked eyes for another second, then Molly shook her head. "Mom...what vans?"

The world suspended for a single moment, like the drawn-out ringing of a bell. Then Molly's eyes flashed out the window, and all the color drained from her face.

Oh crap.

Chapter 12

Julian was already racing down the hall when they reached the bottom of the stairs, sliding his phone back into his pocket with an expression his friends knew all too well.

"There's trouble," he announced without preamble, focusing all his attention on Molly. "I just got off with Rob. There was a prison break at Guilder. A few agents have been attacked."

She stopped dead in her tracks, staring in alarm.

"A prison break?" she repeated incredulously.

In all her years with the agency, such a thing had never happened. Over five hundred years the council had kept a certain breed of criminal locked in the tunnels, not *one* had ever escaped.

Not unless we happened to be imprisoned ourselves.

Julian nodded swiftly, feeling just as shaken himself. "Yeah, I...I only got pieces. He was just arriving at the scene."

Her mind scrambled, trying to keep pace. "A few agents. Which agents?"

His dark eyes flashed to hers.

"The ones who were most resistant to Barnes' cause."

...bloody hell.

"What does that mean?" Eleanor demanded, every muscle in her body on high alert. "Is that someone who works with you? Who is Barnes?"

"He's missing," Julian said softly, his eyes on Molly. "He was last seen walking to the brig."

She took a step back, hands cupping over her mouth.

Considering the ever-widening array of tatùs roaming around the PC tunnels, there were still a few people who wore inhibitors just out of common courtesy when on school grounds. Those who could spread disease, or hear people's thoughts. Those whose ink manifested in such a way that was purely destructive, or were prone to lapses in control.

Cliff Barnes wore an inhibitor. Cliff Barnes was a black hole.

It wasn't just that he was immune to all forms of ink—that was unsettling enough. It was that he could project that immunity outwards, neutralizing every tatù that came into contact.

And no one really knew how far.

The tunnels were given a basic protection by whoever happened to be patrolling at the time, this was in addition to the extensive technological surveillance, but the cells themselves were sealed by nothing more than ink. It was a basic repellant—taken from a retired agent who'd consented to enough experimental blood draws to earn him a celebratory plaque. In essence, his tatù operated like a storm—projecting any magic levelled against it back at the person tenfold.

It was fundamentally unbeatable.

...unless it was projecting immunity.

Molly turned to Julian in horror, as a thousand different implications began to take hold.

If there was one person who could stage a successful prison break, it was the man working in the office just upstairs. And if he was targeting people who'd spoken out against him...?

"He knows about this place," she breathed. "He's read my personnel file, Jules. He's read *all* of our files. I had to file a temporary leave of absence through his office."

The psychic shook his head quickly. "It's fine, that's not—"

"There are vans outside the house."

He stared at her a split second, then his eyes glowed white.

"Oh good heavens…" Eleanor murmured, staggering a step back. One hand lifted to her mouth, as she stared without breathing at his face. "Is he…? Is he all right…?"

Molly ignored her, pelting the psychic with questions. "Can you get a read on Barnes?"

His brow furrowed ever so slightly—half in the present, half in the future. "I'm trying…"

After a few seconds, he shook his head.

"What about my mom?" she insisted, grabbing his arm when he drifted away again. "Or my dad?" She gasped in sudden panic. "Jules, he's in the middle of nowhere—"

He held up a hand, pulling himself free.

"Your dad is fine," he murmured, still awash in that clairvoyant glow. "He's going to stay fine." His head tilted ever so slightly, as he flew through different futures at the speed of light. "And I'm just…just give me a moment…"

What's taking so long? It never takes this long.

Molly flashed a panicked glance out the window before shaking him again.

"What?" she demanded. "You can't see my mom? You can't see the house? You can't see *Scotland*? What is it, Jules?!"

He tranced out a moment longer, then lifted his head. "…I can't see tomorrow."

That's when something crashed through the window.

A split second was all it took for the training to take hold. A split second, triggered by the sound of shattering glass. Molly took a single look at the metal shell rolling on the floor, then she flew forward in a burst of momentum—shouting at the top of her lungs.

"GRENADE!"

The first time she'd seen one had been in a training exercise—the kind of thing that she and Rae had started with the utmost confidence, then instantly regretted gorging themselves on sushi in the hours before. They'd taken off in the opposite direction, thinking that to be the best chance of survival—then were steered patiently back toward it by their trainers. They were not meant to run from these things anymore. They were meant to stop them. And in order to stop a grenade, one needed to use something more than their bare hands.

Without pausing to think, she kicked the thing toward the kitchen, then leapt up on the refrigerator—toppling it over at the same time. The door swung open and it landed squarely atop the explosive, prepared to cushion the worst of the blast. Unable to leap away in time, she simply braced herself for the fallout—watching Julian yank her mother to safety at the same time.

A second passed, then other. Her eyes opened slowly, peering down at the bomb.

Not a bomb, she realized. *A bomb would have detonated already. Which means...*

There was a faint hissing sound, as a thick vapor began rising through the broken door.

"GAS!"

She staggered away from the kitchen, pulling her shirt over her nose and coughing. Julian clapped a hand over her mother's face, and together, they staggered into the hall. The second they were clear of the worst, he yanked out his phone—fingers moving with muscle memory on the keys.

It rang once, then the line opened.

"Hey—"

"Dev!" he shouted, the second he heard his partner's voice. "I'm with Molly at her mom's house in Scotland. There's an unmarked van parked outside, and we're under—"

A bullet fired through the window, knocking the phone out of his hand.

"Shit!" Molly cried, grabbing her mother at the same time. "Get into the basement!"

The three of them sprinted without pause down the back stairway, slamming the door shut behind them and landing in a tangled pile in the center of the floor. While one of them shrank back in terror, the other two made a quick assessment of the room—searching for anything that might be used as a barricade, and anything a little stronger that might be used to fight back. Cleaning supplies, old electronics, tanks of propane meant for camping stoves. Most houses came with a level of basic defensibility, even if the owners were completely unaware at the time.

"It's not ground level," Julian shouted, peering through the three-inch windows with a look of dismay. "Molly, can you get a shot—"

"They're parked on the other side of the house," she interrupted, grabbing hold of a pantry and heaving it up the stairs. "Help me with this."

Together, the two of them blockaded the door and set about securing the windows, ducking every so often as another spray of bullets rained through the glass. He took a piece of shrapnel in the arm, but they kept moving. Another grazed past her cheek, but she'd already ducked in time.

"Mom?" she called over her shoulder. "Talk to me—are you okay?"

Eleanor was slumped against the water-heater in the corner of the room—staring with glassy eyes in no particular direction, as she played back the last several seconds in her mind.

"You jumped on top of it," she answered faintly. "You jumped on top of a bomb."

Molly and Julian exchanged a quick look before returning their focus to the vans.

"Can you see how many there are?" she asked quietly, uncertain what their powers might be.

So far, they'd used nothing but conventional weapons—things more often used in the common world, but there wasn't a doubt in her mind they had ink. For all she knew, it was people she'd worked with. Agents who'd grown a little too attached to Barnes' masochistic cause.

"They've been wearing inhibitors," Julian replied, leaning against the wall as he tried again to see. "But I think there's only two of them. A man and a woman. Nobody that we know."

"Only two?" she panted in reply, wishing desperately that she was armed with anything more than cans of silver polish and ancient bottles of jam. "And he sent them after *us*? I'm insulted."

"Yeah, well...they probably didn't know I was here." Julian flashed her a quick grin before slipping again into the future.

There was a reason their team was so devastatingly effective. Between the unprecedented fire-power and his ability to see what was coming, there were very few things that could stop the famed Kerrigan Gang, especially when someone was foolish enough to corner more than one. But inhibitors worked on everyone alike, and were an equally effective way to level the game. As long as their enemies were wearing them, they couldn't use their powers. But neither could the psychic.

"Come on," he breathed, eyes flickering so quickly that from a distance, it looked like he was having some kind of stroke. "You know you want to. Just show me what I want to—"

He cut off suddenly, his face going pale.

"Molly—"

But by then, it was already too late. The inhibitors had come down and he was able to see every decision that had led to that moment, every agonizing second of their entire plan.

There just wasn't any way to stop it.

There was a flash of light, followed by a faint humming sound. Even after the light vanished, the hum remained. Molly looked up slowly, convinced she'd heard it somewhere before.

"Isn't that—"

Julian slipped out of the future a second later, resurfacing into the present with a gasp.

"It's a force-field," he panted, twisting around to look through the glass. "Just like the one that Brandy uses, but...the guy is hydrokinetic. Molly, they're going to flood the house."

Eleanor straightened up slowly, her eyes flashing from face to face.

"But that's...that's impossible, isn't it?" she asked breathlessly. "Even if they managed to fill it with water—this place is ancient. It would just spill out the sides."

Not if it was contained by that handy little force-field.

The friends shared a quick look, thinking the same thing.

Decades earlier, the same tactic had been used against Devon's father—when he was a young agent in the field. The hydrokinetic then didn't need a force-field to contain it, her control was enough that she could handle that bit herself. But it amounted to the same thing.

Tristan Wardell had almost drowned that day. Right there on dry land.

"We need to get to them first," Julian muttered, having heard the story many times before himself. "If he can channel the water inside, maybe there's a way to break through the barrier."

Without a second thought, he picked up a box-cutter, elbowed open the glass, and hurled it with all his might toward the force-field. There was a faint *ding*, and for a second, they all thought it might have worked. Then it flew back even faster right at his face.

He ducked beneath the broken frame, panting for breath.

"Okay, new plan."

That was when the water began pouring inside.

What started as a trickle, soon grew into a stream, which then turned into a steady flood. In a matter of seconds, it was rushing in through the windows and pooling around their feet—sweeping their legs out from under them and sending random bits of debris floating across the floor.

"Molly?!"

Eleanor let out a panicked shouted, gripping onto the banister for balance. Her daughter spun around and splashed toward her, but by then, the others were having problems themselves.

The lights flickered, then went completely dead—pitching the entire house into sudden darkness. Churning waves of water crashed against the windows with unnatural force, breaking away what remained of the glass and surging in violent tides around their legs. Then it was up to their waists, then it was up to their chests. Then they all shouted in unison as it rose swiftly to their necks.

"We need to get out of here!" Molly gasped, kicking desperately toward the stairs. Her mother was already there, clinging like a panicked cat to the light fixture. Julian was only a step behind her. "We need to get someplace high. Jules, help me with the pantry! It's blocking us—"

There was a mighty crash, as another wave surged inside the house—dragging the psychic backward the second he reached the stairs. Two hands flashed out, reaching desperately for the same banister, but the water wasn't moving the way that water should. There were sudden eddies and rippling currents. It moved first one direction, then another—racing with unnatural strength.

A second later, he was gone. Lost beneath the crashing waves.

"Jules!"

Molly twisted around in a panic, scanning desperately through the chaos. The moon was gone, and the only light they had were the faint beams emanating from the force-field, ones that didn't so much illuminate the darkness, as stretch the shadows with an eerie glow.

She tried ducking her head beneath the water, but it was to no avail. She tried calling out for him again, but the only sound she could hear was the distant rush of current flooding into the house.

This can't be happening! Ten minutes ago, everything was fine!

"JULIAN!"

Her mother's fingers locked around her shoulder in a death-grip, almost as if she sensed what her daughter was going to say next.

"Mom, I've got to go after him," she panted, wrapping both hands around the banister and inching back down into the fast-rising flood. "Start trying to move the pantry, alright? I'll be back in just a moment to help you—"

But there wasn't a need. Because a second later, the psychic reappeared.

"Jules!"

He surfaced with a broken gasp—gulping in deep breaths of air. His skin was pale and his hands were trembling. Strands of dark hair were tangled across his face. A few years ago, he might have found himself at the end of his reserves, but agents of the Privy Council didn't surrender so easily. With a look of pure defiance, he dragged himself slowly up the stairs, one step at a time.

"Are you all right?" Molly gasped, grabbing onto him the second he got close.

"We need to move the pantry," he answered without blinking, picking up right where their conversation had left off. "The current's pushing it backwards, but if we leverage some weight off the ceiling, it should be enough to pull it free."

Molly nodded swiftly, then came to a sudden pause.

"Leverage some weight off the ceiling?" she repeated with a hint of dread.

He nodded grimly.

"We'll have to wait for the water to rise."

Despite the wide array of dangers intelligence operatives were trained to face, there were few things more panicking than the prospect of running out of air. Whether it was drowning, a vacuum-sealed security vault, or good, old fashioned strangulation, it was a lesson that even the best agents took years to get right. Even then, there were certain physical reactions that were beyond one's control. The pounding heartrate, the gasping breaths. The faint tingling that settled into one's lips and extremities—an age-old warning system that things were about to go wrong.

The only thing harder than the situation itself, was willfully allowing it to get worse.

"You mean, we're just going to sit here?" Eleanor screeched, her eyes whipping from one to the other. "We're going to wait until you have just seconds to get it right?"

Julian flashed her a quick look, torn between panic and pity. "It's the only way—"

"And what if it doesn't work?" she demanded, tugging on the pantry herself. From their angle, with the forces leveled against it, the thing didn't budge an inch. "What if it doesn't work, and you don't find out until that water is already over our heads?!"

Molly moved in between them, directly into her line of sight.

"It's *going* to work," she said simply, taking her mother's hands. Her own sense of hysteria was mounting as the water continued to rise, but she forced a steady calm. "It always does."

"But you can't—"

"Trust me," she said softly. "I've done things like this before."

A silent look passed between them, then Eleanor nodded her head.

The only good thing that could be said about their plan, was that they didn't have long to wait. Whether the people outside were over-enthusiastic, or simply nervous about getting seen, the water poured into the house with a new sense of urgency, quickly consuming the stairs.

When it reached the base of the pantry, Julian pulled open the doors and let everything inside spill out into the waves. When the water began to overtake them, the trio stuck their heads inside the hollow space that remained—pulling in a series of gasping breaths.

"This is going to be quick," Julian shouted, raising his voice to be heard about the rushing tide. "When I give the signal, you two are going to grab hold of the banister and duck out of the way. Stay with Molly," he added sharply, slipping into an authoritative tone that Eleanor

Skye hadn't heard since she was a child. "No matter what happens, do NOT let go of Molly's hand."

Molly laced their fingers together, speaking directly into her mother's ear.

"It's going to be all right, mom. Just keep holding onto me, okay?"

Eleanor's head jerked up and down, but she let out a muffled shriek as the water battered against the sides of the pantry. It had almost overtaken it by now, filling up every corner of the room. At the last possible moment, she turned to Molly—eyes wide with fright.

"I don't suppose," she faltered and started again, "I don't suppose there's a chance your father organized this as well? Part of his endless attempt to encourage mother-daughter bonding?"

Molly's lips parted in astonishment, then she flashed the world's most unlikely smile.

"I think that's *exactly* what happened."

The two let out a burst of hysterical laughter, fighting to keep their heads above the water in the ever-shrinking space. Then Julian let out a sudden shout, and they ducked beneath the waves.

Total. Consuming. Darkness.

Molly clamped down on her mother's hand, wrapping the crook of her elbow around the banister at the same time. She hadn't counted on the darkness, though at this point, she should have seen it coming. While the force-field generated enough distant light to illuminate whatever remained of the basement, the swirling eddies kept those precious rays out of reach.

She felt her mother's fingers tighten. The woman had no training and was already running out of breath. Somewhere above them, Julian was braced against the ceiling, both arms heaving desperately against the pantry—prying the thing loose with all his incredible might.

What if it doesn't work, she wondered suddenly, allowing herself to stray down a line of thinking that had been long silenced by her years in the field. *What if this is it? What if after all this time, after all these years of fighting, I finally reconcile with my mother only to immediately get her killed?*

Her hand squeezed harder, as she was suddenly flooded with a thousand things she wished that she had said. Silly stories she would have like to have shared, or little reassurances about the nature of her job that seemed wildly preposterous when considered in the current moment.

She wanted to say each one of them. If they made it through this, she vowed she would do it right there on the spot. Then just when she thought that she might never get the chance, there was a sudden movement somewhere above them, as the pantry finally gave way.

The door burst open a second later, and the trio was swept with a rush of water onto the floor of the house. They spilled without a hint of coordination across the living room, tumbling into chairs and over furniture before crashing to a stop against the far wall. The urge to simply rip open the front door or leap out one of the broken windows was overwhelming. For a split second, three pairs of eyes shot involuntarily toward each of the exits, moved with the feral need to escape.

But there were people waiting outside with semi-automatic weapons. And while they might actually make it to dry land, it wouldn't be any escape. That force-field was still covering the house like a dome, sealing in all the water. They would only be prolonging the inevitable.

Not that we have a better plan.

"You don't happen to have any weapons in the house, do you Mrs. Skye?" Julian asked hopefully, pushing upward as the water poured around his feet. "Maybe some...guns and ammo?"

It was a stilted question, asked with just enough hesitancy to catch the woman's focus. For a split second, she froze with a blank stare. Then she threw up her arms in sudden understanding.

"That was just a stupid magazine," she exclaimed. "It was delivered here by mistake! Do you guys really think I've been keeping an arsenal of weapons hidden somewhere on the premises?"

They wisely chose not to answer, turning to each other instead.

"It wouldn't have helped, anyway," Molly murmured. "You saw how fast that box-cutter flew back at you. Do you really want to try the same thing with a gun?"

He pushed back his hair, scanning quickly around the house.

"Just feels better to have something in my hands..."

I hear that.

Molly's eyes flashed out the window, as the raging current began to slowly fill the next layer of the house. A flicker of voltage was crackling just beneath the surface, aching to be let free.

"Don't even think about it," he warned swiftly, as the electric glow stirred restlessly in the backs of her eyes. "We're inside a sealed dome that's filling with water. *Electricity* is not the answer."

"Then what is?" she asked quietly, taking quick stock of the situation as the trio started backing instinctively toward the stairs. "We'll go up to the attic and what then? We're going to find ourselves in exactly the same situation, only this time, there won't be a new set of stairs to climb."

His eyes flashed white for the briefest of moments before he shook his head helplessly, grabbing both women by the wrist and towing them swiftly down the hall.

"I don't know, Skye. We'll figure it out on the way."

There was something utterly surreal about seeing a house fill up with water. Something that went beyond the usual flares of—*someone's trying to kill us*—and played strange, dreamlike tricks on the mind. They hadn't made it to the second story, before the living room furniture started floating, before those pictures that framed the hallways lifted off their nails and began drifting away. The pillows sank, the floorboards shimmered, and by the time they reached the landing, a sea of watery faces was staring up at them—dozens of memories, caught in suspension, watching them flee.

"My wedding book," Eleanor whispered suddenly, pausing beside her. "My purse and credit cards. Birth certificates, travel documents...they're all going to be swept away."

Molly flashed her a look, then gave her hand a quick squeeze.

"We can conjure new ones," she comforted quietly, watching as her mother's prized curtains began swirling in the rising tide. "Even the pictures. Rae can see them in your mind, exactly as they were, then create new ones of thin air. Nothing we lose today will be permanent."

Except perhaps our lives.

Eleanor nodded once, then pursed her lips with a frown. "She can...*conjure* new ones? I thought you said Rae could turn invisible."

Julian cast them a quick look, but said nothing, as Molly's cheeks flamed bright as her hair.

It wasn't the easiest thing in the world—explaining someone like Rae Kerrigan. Especially to someone averse to magic. In an effort to make her seem more approachable, she might have latched onto the least-threatening power she could imagine and made it seem like that was the only one.

"That's a conversation best saved for later." Unable to meet her mother's eyes, she took her hand instead—bounding toward the next set of stairs. "No time now—we've got to run!"

There wasn't anything exceptionally defensible about the attic, it was simply the highest place in the house they were able to climb. The second they burst through the door and slid to a stop, the helplessness of their predicament set in all over again and hysteria began to take hold.

"So what now?" Eleanor demanded, throwing up her hands. She was drenched to the bone, but a strand of wilted pearls was still clinging to her neck. "We climb onto the roof?"

"The roof would never hold us," Julian muttered, stuffing some metal paneling beneath the crack in the door, "for a multitude of reasons. And I highly doubt we could make it outside."

He was right.

Molly pressed her face to the window, shocked to see that the force-field wasn't a dome as she'd originally envisioned, but merely a wrap that clung to the entire length of the house. From the inside, it looked like they'd been coated in tissue paper. The kind that didn't allow one to breathe.

"It's close," she murmured to herself. "I didn't realize it was so close."

Julian stood up behind her, stepping back to assess his work.

"That's the best I can manage, but it won't hold the water for long. And it doesn't matter if Devon took off in the jet the second I called him, back-up is still at least thirty minutes away."

At least.

For all they knew, Devon wasn't even on campus when he got the call. Or perhaps the jet had already been sequestered for another mission, tracking down all those escaped convicts.

"It's right against the window," Molly continued in a low murmur, never taking her eyes from the glass. "If I opened it up, I could actually touch it."

The psychic threw a quick glance over his shoulder.

"Here's an idea—*don't* do that. Help me find a way out of this."

She stared a moment longer, then took a sudden step back.

"I think I already have." The others looked over at the same time as she pointed a finger to the glass. "Jules, *you* can break the force-field."

There was a pause.

"Damn, you're lazy—"

"I'm serious," she interrupted, bringing him closer. "My power is useless in here, but yours isn't. You can make a psychic connection and use it to break us free."

His face stilled without a hint of expression.

"...how?"

Now that the idea had been planted, it was quick to take hold. She pulled him even closer, taking hold of both his wrists as she stared up at him, talking at the speed of light.

"I know that's not how it's intended to be used, but we've stretched our ink for things like that before, and Jules—there isn't anything stronger. Rae's sun-fire is the only thing that's remotely comparable, and at this range, that would probably burn us all alive."

Eleanor paled in the background, unseen by the others.

"Yeah, Molly, but *how*?" he said again. "Make a psychic connection? With what? And how the hell is something like that supposed to break us free?"

Her eyes glowed with excitement, latching onto this single shred of hope.

"When you did it with Gabriel in Iceland, Dev said the force when you two broke apart was enough to throw you into the wall. I've seen you squeeze through tables and pull the doors off cars when your mind is like that. It's a hundred times better than a strength tatù, it could actually work!"

He shook his head slowly, looking profoundly uncertain.

"So you want me to...what? Push through it?"

The paneling beneath the door was a good stop-gap, but torrents of water were already leaking through. They seeped through the cracks and bubbled up through the floorboards, coating the floor of the attic like an ever-rising pane of glass.

"Exactly," Molly said quickly, watching as the level rose slowly up the wall. "Make a connection, let that power build, then have a hand resting against it when you break apart."

His eyes flashed to hers.

"And if they *shoot* me in the meantime?"

That's a good question.

She paused a split second, then fluttered her fingers with a vengeful smile. "If they do that, they'll need to lower the force-field. And if they do *that*—I will shock them straight into hell."

This part, he didn't question. He'd seen such things with his own eyes. It was the rest of it that was throwing him. Particularly the part where he fixed the problem with a wave of his hand.

"But none of those times were intentional," he muttered in a panic. "I wasn't even aware they'd happened until they were already done. And even if I could...what am I supposed to connect with? The second that field comes down—you're going to need to hit them with everything you've got. You can't do anything like that if you're psychically tied to me."

Now it was her turn to pause.

He was absolutely right. To forge a psychic connection was one of the most depleting and excruciating things a person could do. The few people who'd attempted it with Julian before had been scarred for life—unwilling to ever attempt such a thing again. The psychic himself avoided it whenever possible. Saving it for bigger things like changing the future, or saving the world.

Or imminent drowning. We'll add that to the list.

"I could..." She trailed off, trying desperately to think as the water rose to her knees. As if the inevitable creep of it wasn't enough, it was also breathtakingly cold. "Well, maybe if we—"

"Oh, for heaven's sake," Eleanor interrupted. "Just do it with me."

The others turned to her in unison, unwilling to commit either way.

"It's...it's *incredibly* painful, Mom."

"And incredibly dangerous," Julian added nervously, eyeing the water as well. "And it's not like I could stop once we'd gotten started. That would be our only shot."

"It's a lot better than drowning in my attic!"

Without waiting for them to either agree or disagree, she seized his hand, then grabbed hold of the window. The latch flipped free, and the strange hum of the force-field pulsed through the glass, ticking down the seconds remaining where any of them could breathe.

"Come on," Eleanor commanded, squaring her shoulders. "It's now or never."

It sounded crazy. It probably *was* crazy.

But it was also the only chance they had.

Julian cast a final look at Molly—like he was seeking permission, like he was seeking forgiveness—then he stepped forward and took Eleanor's other hand.

"Take a breath," he said softly.

There was no warning beyond that.

At precisely the same moment, their eyes sealed shut and their heads snapped down to their chests. Eleanor didn't scream, they had to give her that. But her mouth was open and twisted with such horror, it was an expression her daughter would never be able to forget. Julian took it in better stride, though his entire body flinched as though he'd been struck. Within a few seconds, the lines that surrounded him blurred and a celestial glow began to envelop his entire body—clinging to his dark hair like a halo and lifting him several inches off his feet.

Molly took a step closer as the water rose to her waist.

It wasn't until that very moment that she realized what was happening. She'd been so focused on the aftershock, on the logistical components, that she forgot what the psychic and her mother were actually about to do. A look of frozen curiosity stole across her features as her gaze drifted between them—wondering what was happening behind those sleeping eyes.

Then the water swelled to her chest, and she guided Julian's hand to the window—taking a firm grip herself on the frame. There was no way to reach him, and no way to know when he was ready. She could only hope he'd get there quickly, as the water inched toward her neck.

"Come on," she whispered, lifting her chin. "Come on."

It was bizarre to be the only one who could feel it, the only one who seemed to notice that all three of them were about to drown. Her eyes dilated in fright and she sucked in little breaths, trying to keep herself together, trying to keep their heads lifted as well.

Then all at once, it happened.

A vibration rippled through Julian, unlike anything she'd ever felt. It wasn't hot, exactly. But something about it made it feel like she was going to burn her hand. She ripped down the frame and pressed his palm to the force-field, giving it a direction, giving it somewhere to aim.

Then came the shockwave, bursting like a nova in the night.

It shattered the force-field upon impact, leaving the stench of ozone in its wake. The entire house shook like a tree in a storm, and a pair of distant voices shouted down below.

Then came the lightning, ripping like a dagger through the sky.

It struck both of the people for whom it was intended, carving a home in their chests, before bursting through to the other side. They were still gazing upward in wonder, the air was still ringing with shouts of belated surprise. Then they dropped heavy to their knees, never to rise again.

Then came the flood.

Considering how desperate they were to escape their magical binding, the friends had never paused to consider what might actually happen if they were to make it out alive. Then water stayed standing for a split second longer, hovering in an impossible column against the night sky. Then with a *crash* that would continue to puzzle the residents of Evanton for years to come, it collapsed like a punctured balloon, spilling the remnants of the house across the shadowy grass.

The friends spilled right along with it—thankfully bypassing the worst of the wreckage, as the tide of water coming down from the attic rushed them straight down the stairs. The front door was already gone, and they tumbled into the front lawn along with all the rest.

Not one of them was moving. Not one of them was even conscious. Then very slowly, after several rather pathetic false starts, the one lying in the middle opened her eyes.

Oh shit...

She stared up at what remained of her mother's house, the meticulously-crafted Scottish cottage that had taken so much of her time. The walls were sagging, the interior was drenched, even the frame itself was standing crooked, like the whole thing could be taken down by even the slightest breeze. Oddly enough, the only thing that remained perfectly intact was her mother's vanity; a poetic anomaly that she'd spend a great deal of time thinking about in the weeks to come.

"Mom?"

She scrambled across the wet grass to Eleanor's side, pausing only to locate Julian and check his wrist for a pulse as she flew by. The psychic was alive and breathing. Her mother—she wasn't so sure.

"Mom!"

She dropped quickly onto the grass beside her, lifting her head carefully off the lawn. Her eyes were closed, but she thought she could feel a faint heartbeat. Upon closer inspection, she was fairly sure she saw the traces of an even fainter scowl.

"Molly Elizabeth Skye...what have you done to my house?"

The woman's eyes fluttered slowly open, and Molly let out a sigh of relief, ignoring the usual stiffness they held between them and gathering her up in a tight embrace. Eleanor winced ever so slightly, then her face relaxed into an unseen smile. A hand came up, stroking her daughter's hair.

"You did it," she murmured, smoothing the damp strands. "I never doubted you could." Her eyes strayed a little farther to where Julian was stirring in the grass. "Is everyone all right?"

Molly squeezed her tighter, unable to let go. "Everyone that needs to be."

They held on for another moment, still coming down from the shock, then a precarious creak behind them made them both whirl around—watching as the cottage drooped to the side.

They stared in silence, then turned back to each other.

"Sorry about the house," Molly whispered.

Her mother regarded her with a little smile. "You know what? I never liked that house."

Chapter 13

The best thing to say in memorial to the Skye family's deceased home, was that it had been out in the country. Far enough away, that no one noticed when it transformed into a quivering pillar of water and spilled all over the Scottish moor. Far enough away, that no one was able to distinguish between the sound of thunder, and the deafening arrival of a supersonic jet.

Molly's eyes drifted open as it passed overhead, following sleepily along as it made a quick circle to sweep the terrain, then performed an emergency landing in the middle of a field.

Three figures hopped onto the grass, racing toward them.

"Head's up," she murmured, hoisting onto her elbows. "We've got company."

At some point since the *dissolution of the manor*, as it would later come to be called, each of the friends had woken up, mumbled a few words, then fallen back to sleep. Eleanor and Julian were in a particularly bad state, having participated in a cosmic bond, but they sat up when she called.

Devon reached them first, appearing suddenly on the lawn. "Is everybody okay?!"

By now, most of Molly's friends knew better than to 'flaunt' their powers in front of her mother, but he made no effort to check his speed. In a blur of color, he flashed between the women, checking for damages—before helping his partner delicately to his feet.

"You missed the show," Julian greeted him wearily, still bleeding from where a piece of glass had wedged itself into his arm. "It was one for the books."

Devon took him gently by the shoulder, tearing open his sleeve. "Oh yeah?" His eyes flashed across the lawn to the two bodies crumbled in the grass. "And I was so hoping to catch the second act."

The two men locked eyes for a moment, then Julian shook his head. They were gone, struck dead by the voltage. It was a fact that Eleanor was piecing together for the first time.

"Oh my..." She trailed off, pointing a trembling hand. "You don't think...?"

The friends followed her gaze, mouths thinning into a hard line.

Rae appeared a second later, a cloud of raven hair blowing ahead of her when she screeched to a sudden stop. She'd been the one flying the jet—not trusting Devon to do it himself—and a pair of oversized headphones were still dangling on a severed cord from her neck.

"Is everybody okay?!"

Molly smiled to herself as she echoed the exact words her husband had gasped just a few seconds before. It was hardly a rarity. She wondered if they knew how often they did that.

Lacking the energy to say the words aloud, she spoke them clearly in her mind.

'We're fine, Rae. But my mom's freaking out. Can you distract her from the bodies?'

The two girls locked eyes for a split second, then Rae nodded ever so slightly—pacing casually across the grass and coming to a deliberate stop in front of her mother.

"Hey, Mrs. Skye. How are you feeling?"

"Molly!"

Molly lifted her head as the third figure streaked toward the house, slowing down ever so slightly when he saw the dilapidated remains, before catching her in a bone-shattering hug.

She grinned in spite of herself, rocking back and forth.

"Hey, honey."

Luke kissed her fiercely on both cheeks before pulling back to examine her. Despite the fact that she was awake and talking, those blue eyes were wild with worry, locking desperately onto hers.

"We were so afraid something terrible had happened," he murmured, cupping both sides of her face before kissing her again. "The phone went dead just as Jules was calling—"

"Yeah, somebody shot it out of his hand." Her eyes flickered from the house to the distant vans, still parked innocently along the drive. "It's been a bit of a day."

Right on cue, Devon detached himself from the others and began storming that way himself, pulling a gun from his jacket as he did. Their attackers were gone, and according to the psychic, he wasn't going to find any more of them. But a part of him secretly hoped that Julian was wrong.

"Where are the kids?" Molly asked softly, staring after him.

Luke tightened his grip, clasping her to his chest. "We left them with Angel and Gabriel," he replied. "Beth was already on her way."

That was how Molly knew it was serious.

She pulled back then, studying his face as well. It was a trick they'd picked up over the years, learning to read the little details so the person wouldn't have to relive any unnecessary trauma themselves. It was the reason Devon had simply tended Julian's arm instead of asking first thing what had happened. It was the reason Rae was putting aside her concerns and tending to her mom.

That being said, things had escalated a good deal past that point.

"How bad is it?"

"It's bad," Luke answered bluntly. "Lots of agents are gone—turned in their notice the same morning and fell completely off the grid. Lots of agents are missing—some of them never checked in from the field, some of them never showed up in places they were supposed to be. I'd hoped if this ended up happening, it would be mostly contained within the PC, but that message of Barnes' was universal, and there's a pretty clear spread across the board."

She shook her head slowly, unable to believe things had progressed so far. "How's your dad handling it?"

His lips quirked in a hard smile. "He's taking roll."

Devon returned a moment later, pacing toward them with the unsatisfied look of someone who'd both uncovered nothing and never got the opportunity to fire his gun.

"The vans were clean," he declared. "No papers, no prints. I'm having the office run their plates now, but ten pounds says they'll have been stolen from a parking garage near the airport. This wasn't some opportunistic assault. They worked things out in advance. They made a proper plan."

Julian stretched out his arms, strands of damp hair falling around his face.

"Well, that's Barnes, isn't it? The man who sits at the desk. The man who knows all the plans." His dark eyes strayed back across the field, falling on the remains of the house. "This might not have been spontaneous, but Molly put in her leave less than four days ago. Either it happened to coincide with the prison break, or someone has been planning this for a very long time."

Why not take a while to plan? We gave him a long time.

Molly shook her head slowly, folding her arms with a shiver across her chest. So many times they had discussed the 'Barnes problem.' So many times, they'd come up blank.

The trouble was, they couldn't just enforce their opinion on the rest of the supernatural community. Even if they were in the majority. Even if they were right. They had faced enough backlash in the wake of the Vivian scandal in terms of nepotism and the potential of a magical oligarchy rising up to take control. They must be tolerant. Discussion was to be encouraged.

Until it leads to a prison break.

"I don't know what I'm supposed to..." Eleanor trailed off, wringing her hands together as she gazed over the remnants of her house. "I don't know what I'm supposed to do. Your father will be home in a few days. At least, he would...if there was a home to come back to."

Molly lifted her eyes guiltily, but Rae stepped immediately to her side.

"You'll stay with my mother," she said easily. "She's just a few hours down the coast."

Eleanor turned to her in shock.

Despite the countless hours they'd spent enduring each other's company, she had cooled significantly on her daughter's best friend, when it turned out that Rae Kerrigan was the fount of all things magical and dangerous and strange. Since then, the two had maintained a careful truce. One that most certainly did *not* extend, to open invitations visiting each other's homes.

"Are you sure?" Eleanor asked tentatively.

Are you sure? Molly echoed immediately in her mind.

"Of course," Rae answered without hesitation. "I figure you don't want to spend the next few weeks in London, and this way, you can stay in the vicinity while I round up a couple of fellow conjurers to fix the damage on the house."

It continued stubbornly wilting behind her.

"Or maybe just replace the entire house," she amended, wincing apologetically as another window shattered onto the lawn. "I'm sorry for the hassle, Mrs. Skye. But rest assured, none of the neighbors will know anything ever happened. You have my personal assurance of that."

"Please, call me Eleanor."

The woman gave her a grateful squeeze before turning back to her daughter. The endless night was almost over. There were hints of dawn at the edges of the sky.

"So I guess this finally solves the question of why it's so difficult to get you to visit," she said with a half-hearted smile. "You're a nightmare, sweetheart. Chaos follows wherever you go."

A few days earlier, Molly might have cringed. Now, she flashed a mischievous grin.

"You have to admit...it keeps things interesting."

Eleanor let out a breath of laughter. "It certainly does."

They stood there a while longer, watching as Luke jogged back across the grass and fired up the jet, then without a hint of warning, her mother pulled her into another embrace.

"Let me just say something," she said quietly, "and I don't want you to make a big deal about it, and I don't want to ever talk about it again."

Molly stiffened, prepared for the worst. "...okay."

Eleanor's arms tightened. "I'm so very proud of you, darling."

Molly closed her eyes, grinning into her neck. "Thanks Mom."

The breeze picked up around them, tangling their crimson hair.

"I've never been able to figure out this perfume," she continued suddenly, leaning closer to give it another sniff. "It's so familiar, that sweetness. But I can never place it."

Eleanor pulled back in surprise. "Oh—you don't recognize it? It's ginger-berries. You used to love them when you were a child. A little too sweet for my tastes, to be honest. But they never failed to calm you down."

Molly stared back at her, stunned to the core.

"So you decided to wear them? You seeped them into your perfume?"

Eleanor regarded her for a moment before wiping a trace of soot from her face. "Don't be ridiculous, darling. I had it specially made."

THE FLIGHT BACK HOME was quick and uneventful. Half the party silently fumed that they hadn't gotten there earlier, while the other half drooled in their sleep.

By the time they touched back down in London, the sun was just rising over the misty peaks.

Beth was waiting for them at the house and Benji was waving excitedly by her side. He ran to his mother, giving her a quick hug—before leaping upon Eleanor with a delighted shout.

"Finally—you're here!" he exclaimed. "I've got so many adventures planned!"

Her eyebrows raised with a smile, as Beth transferred him carefully into her arms.

"You do?" she asked with mock seriousness. "Well, you're in luck, young man. Because I've come here looking for an adventure. And you might be just the person I need to see..."

The two of them vanished inside—presumably so Eleanor could critique the penthouse and inspire/traumatize the adoring doorman—while Luke followed behind them with a grin.

"This is going to be interesting..."

Molly flashed a grin. "Oh, it's going to be a lot worse than that." She took a step to follow him, then stopped just as fast—glancing back at the psychic wandering down the street. "I'll catch up with you, okay?"

"Sure."

He pressed a kiss to her cheek, and watched as she hurried quickly down the sidewalk, catching the psychic by surprise before falling into pace beside his long strides.

"So I never got a chance to thank you," she murmured, "for everything that happened, for flying out all that way. I think my mom's officially inviting you to Christmas."

He let out a breath of laughter, eyes locked on the door of his house. "I'd be delighted...if she'll be here in London."

Molly giggled, slipping under his arm. "Fair enough."

They walked just a short way further, coming to a stop at the walkway to his house. She expected him to go straight inside, but he paused—turning around to face her.

"You know," he began carefully, "a psychic connection isn't something to take lightly. No matter what we were trying to accomplish, I saw pretty deep inside your mom's head."

Molly shuddered in spite of herself. "I'm so sorry. Maybe there's a way you can start seeing Angel's therapist. After everything you went through, Luke and I are more than happy to foot the bill—"

He silenced her with a parting embrace, pressing a kiss to her forehead. "That woman loves you, Molly Elizabeth. She loves you more than life itself."

She stared up at him in shock as the door swung open behind him and a lovely woman stepped onto the porch. A woman whose eyes warmed when they swept over her bedraggled husband, lingering on his *The Highlands Welcome You* sweatshirt.

"Have a fun trip?" she asked lightly, as he paced into the house.

He flashed a rueful grin.

"Not a word, Angie. Not a single word."

He vanished a moment later, probably heading upstairs to see Lily, while Molly lifted her hand in an apologetic wave. "Thanks for letting me borrow him."

To her surprise, Angel lingered on the porch.

"It's no problem. How did it go with your mom?"

There was a pause.

"You mean besides the fact that I let supernatural assassins capsize her house?"

Angel nodded without expression. "Did that make her pretty mad?"

Molly laughed in spite of herself, bowing her head with a grin. No matter how many books she read, or movies she watched, or pedestrians she casually stalked in an effort to 'study the nuances of human behavior,' there was something about Angel that never quite fit in with the rest.

"We've reached a détente. I'm calling it progress."

Angel nodded again, regarding her with a thoughtful expression. "You want to hear something strange?" she asked abruptly. "When I first joined up with the council, slipped into this world, everyone thought I'd be so threatened by Rae. She was always the one moving the players, the one calling the shots. But it was never Rae. It was always you."

Molly froze on the sidewalk, staring back in surprise. "Me?" she repeated incredulously. "Why would you say that?"

Angel's face softened with a little smile. "You mean the world to him. Always have, always will. He looks up to you, I think. You were actually the reason he decided to have children."

If Molly was shocked before, she was flat-out astonished now. Not just at the things she was hearing, but that they were coming from Angel—a girl not prone to such revelations.

"I never knew that," she answered carefully. "I thought Lily was a surprise."

"She was," Angel answered easily. "We certainly weren't planning on it. But the last time we talked before the pregnancy...things had changed. He figured if you were willing to do it with Benji, after everything you'd seen, maybe there was some hope in it after all. Maybe it was worth the risk."

Molly stood there for a moment, trying to process. Then her lips curved into a slow smile. "You know what...?" She glanced back at the house, eyes twinkling in the early light. "I think you're right."

THE END

The Chronicles of Gabriel

GABRIEL ALDEN WAS LIVING the fairytale.

He'd replaced his childhood ghosts with a lovably neurotic family. The shadows that chased him were finally laid to rest. He'd adopted a son and was about to marry the girl of his dreams.

So why did he keep waiting for the other shoe to drop? Probably because it always does.

After a prison break from the heart of the Privy Council, the supernatural community is shaken to the core. Despite Carter's insistence that everything is business as usual, agents are still being targeted, Barnes' forces are growing, and it's impossible to know who to trust.

In the days leading up to his wedding, Gabriel finds himself questioning all kinds of things he'd believed to be certain. Can a person with his history make a decent father? Can he learn to operate within the same ethical boundaries as the others? Will his compass ever point true north, or will it always be a little skewed?

Sometimes happily ever after is only the beginning...

JULIAN'S COVER QUESTION

There is a reason why the cover is unique for "Julian" than what readers expected. You'll have to read Julian's story to find out why.

However, I wanted to share a sneak peek into the original cover so readers can have some fun and try to figure out what's going on. Join me on my FB page, fan page or Instagram for clues and comments to be included in the conversation!

Here's the peek at the original cover... (one more page turn lol)

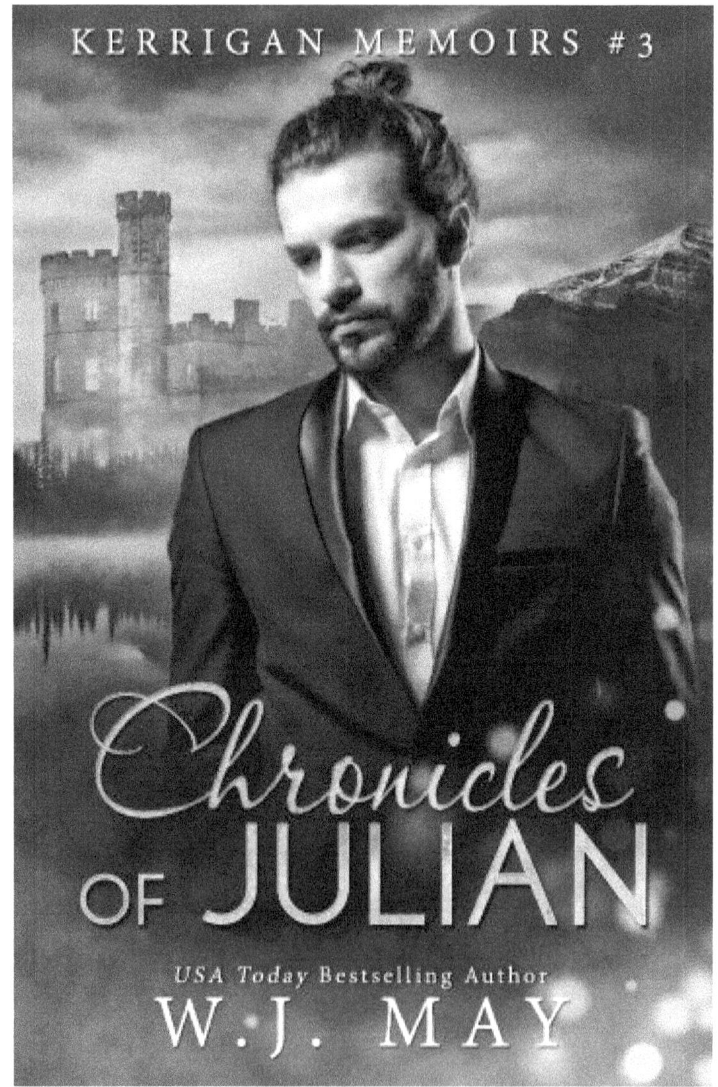
KERRIGAN MEMOIRS #3
Chronicles OF JULIAN
USA Today Bestselling Author
W.J. MAY

The Chronicles of:
Devon
Angel
Julian
Molly
Gabriel
Rae

TUDOR COMPARISON:

Aumbry Hall –A recess to hold sacred vessels, often found in castle chapels.

Aumbry House was considered very special to hold the female students - their sacred vessels (especially Rae Kerrigan).

Joist Hall – A timber stretched from wall-to-wall to support floorboards.

Joist House was considered a building of support where the male students could support and help each other.

Oratory –A private chapel in a house.

Private education room in the school where the students were able to practice their gifting and improve their skills. Also used as a banquet - dance hall when needed.

Oriel –A projecting window in a wall; originally a form of porch, often of wood. The original bay windows of the Tudor period. Guilder College majority of windows were oriel.

Rae often felt her life was being watching through one of these windows. Hence the constant reference to them.

Refectory –A communal dining hall. Same termed used in Tudor times.

Scriptorium –A Medieval writing room in which scrolls were also housed.

Used for English classes and still store some of the older books from the Tudor reign (regarding tatùs).

Privy Council –Secret council and "arm of the government" similar to the CIA, etc.... In Tudor times, the Privy Council was King Henry's board of advisors and helped run the country.

Find W.J. May

Website:
https://www.wjmaybooks.com
Facebook:
https://www.facebook.com/pages/Author-WJ-May-FAN-PAGE/
141170442608149
Newsletter:
SIGN UP FOR W.J. May's Newsletter to find out about new releases, updates, cover reveals and even freebies!
http://www.wjmaybooks.com/subscribe

Book I - *Rae of Hope* is FREE!
Book Trailer:
http://www.youtube.com/watch?v=gILAwXxx8MU
Book II - *Dark Nebula*
Book Trailer:
http://www.youtube.com/watch?v=Ca24STi_bFM
Book III - *House of Cards*
Book IV - *Royal Tea*
Book V - *Under Fire*
Book VI - *End in Sight*
Book VII – *Hidden Darkness*
Book VIII – *Twisted Together*
Book IX – *Mark of Fate*
Book X – *Strength & Power*
Book XI – *Last One Standing*
BOOK XII – *Rae of Light*

PREQUEL –

Christmas Before the Magic
Question the Darkness
Into the Darkness
Fight the Darkness
Alone the Darkness
Lost the Darkness

W.J. May
THE CHRONICLES
OF KERRIGAN
SEQUEL
A Matter OF TIME
Time PIECE
Second CHANCE
Glitch IN TIME
Our TIME
Precious TIME

SEQUEL –

Matter of Time
Time Piece
Second Chance
Glitch in Time
Out Time
Precious Time

The Chronicles of Kerrigan: Gabriel

Living in the Past

Present for Today

Staring at the Future

More books by W.J. May

Hidden Secrets Saga:
Download Seventh Mark part 1 For FREE
Book Trailer:
http://www.youtube.com/watch?v=Y-_vVYC1gvo

LIKE MOST TEENAGERS, Rouge is trying to figure out who she is and what she wants to be. With little knowledge about her past, she has questions but has never tried to find the answers. Everything changes when she befriends a strangely intoxicating family. Siblings Grace and Michael, appear to have secrets which seem connected to Rouge. Her hunch is confirmed when a horrible incident occurs at an outdoor party. Rouge may be the only one who can find the answer.

An ancient journal, a Sioghra necklace and a special mark force life-altering decisions for a girl who grew up unprepared to fight for her life or others.

All secrets have a cost and Rouge's determination to find the truth can only lead to trouble...or something even more sinister.

RADIUM HALOS - THE SENSELESS SERIES
Book 1 is FREE:

Everyone needs to be a hero at one point in their life.

The small town of Elliot Lake will never be the same again.

Caught in a sudden thunderstorm, Zoe, a high school senior from Elliot Lake, and five of her friends take shelter in an abandoned uranium mine. Over the next few days, Zoe's hearing sharpens drastically, beyond what any normal human being can detect. She tells her friends, only to learn that four others have an increased sense as well. Only Kieran, the new boy from Scotland, isn't affected.

Fashioning themselves into superheroes, the group tries to stop the strange occurrences happening in their little town. Muggings, break-ins, disappearances, and murder begin to hit too close to home. It leads the team to think someone knows about their secret - someone who wants them all dead.

An incredulous group of heroes. A traitor in the midst. Some dreams are written in blood.

Courage Runs Red

The Blood Red Series
Book 1 is FREE

WHAT IF COURAGE WAS your only option?

When Kallie lands a college interview with the city's new hot-shot police officer, she has no idea everything in her life is about to change. The detective is young, handsome and seems to have an unnatural ability to stop the increasing local crime rate. Detective Liam's particular interest in Kallie sends her heart and head stumbling over each other.

When a raging blood feud between vampires' spills into her home, Kallie gets caught in the middle. Torn between love and family loyalty she must find the courage to fight what she fears the most and possibly risk everything, even if it means dying for those she loves.

Daughter of Darkness - Victoria
Only Death Could Stop Her Now
The Daughters of Darkness is a series of female heroines who may or may not know each other, but all have the same father, Vlad Montour.
Victoria is a Hunter Vampire

Don't miss out!

Visit the website below and you can sign up to receive emails whenever W.J. May publishes a new book. There's no charge and no obligation.

https://books2read.com/r/B-A-SSF-NEAXB

Did you love *Chronicles of Molly*? Then you should read *Royal Factions Box Set Books #1-3*[1] by W.J. May!

Book 1 - The Price for Peace

How do you keep fighting when you've already been claimed?

When sixteen-year-old Elise is ripped from her home and taken to the royal palace as a permanent 'guest', she thinks her life is over.

Little does she know it has only just begun...

After befriending a group of other captives, including the head-strong Will, Elise finds herself swept away to a world she never knew existed—polished, sculpted, and refined until she can hardly recognize her own reflection. She should be happy to have escaped the poverty of her former life. But she knows a dark truth.

The palace is a dream on the surface, but a nightmare underneath.

---

1. https://books2read.com/u/mYGyvY

2. https://books2read.com/u/mYGyvY

With a dwindling population, the royals have imprisoned the teenagers to marry and breed. Only seven days remain of freedom before they will be selected by a courtier and forever claimed.

Danger lurks around every corner. The only chance of escape is death.

But when the day of the claiming finally arrives...the world will never be the same.

<u>Book 2 - The Cost for Surviving</u>

Is it really living when you spend your life in a cage...

The wait is over, the dust has settled, and the captives have finally been claimed. Elise thought the deadly game was finished, but the more time she spends in the palace, the more she begins to fear the real game has only just begun.

In the aftermath of the ceremony, each of the friends try to adjust to their new life. But some are having more trouble than others. Will's perpetual defiance lands him in trouble with the queen herself, while Elise is playing a dangerous balancing act, trying to understand the affections of the prince. The man can be sweet, but also psychotic. At times, he seems to truly care—but with a snap of his fingers, she'd be sentenced to death.

Danger is brewing. In the royal court, nothing is as it seems. They are told repeatedly to content themselves with the life for which they've been chosen. But how can you live with monsters without becoming a monster yourself? Is it really a life, or just going through the motions?

The more time they spend in the palace, the longer the days drag on, the more a single word keeps rising in each of their minds...escape.

<u>Book 3 - The Punishment for Deception</u>

How can you move on with the future without surrendering the past?

When an escape attempt goes desperately awry, Elise and Will find themselves at the mercy of the very people who have imprisoned them all this time. Tensions sharpen, punishments are severe, and they soon discover what terrible things are required if they wish to survive.

But such wild spirits were never meant to be tamed.

While appearing to submit, the future princess still dreams of freedom. And as the day of her wedding approaches, those dreams begin to turn into something more.

With so many eyes upon her, can she maintain the illusion? Is the crown prince really such a monster, or is there more to him than meets the eye?

Time is running out. All that's left are choices.

But will she have the strength to decide?

Royal Factions

The Price for Peace – Book 1The Cost for Surviving – Book 2The Punishment for Deception – Book 3Faking Perfection – Book 4The Most Cherished – Book 5The Strength to Endure – Book 6

Read more at www.wjmaybooks.com.

Also by W.J. May

Beginning's End Series
Beginnings
Curiosity
Scrutiny
Foresight

Blood Red Series
Courage Runs Red
The Night Watch
Marked by Courage
Forever Night
The Other Side of Fear
Blood Red Box Set Books #1-5

Daughters of Darkness: Victoria's Journey
Victoria
Huntress
Coveted (A Vampire & Paranormal Romance)
Twisted
Daughter of Darkness - Victoria - Box Set

Great Temptation Series
The Devil's Footsteps
Heaven's Command
Mortals Surrender

Hidden Secrets Saga
Seventh Mark - Part 1
Seventh Mark - Part 2
Marked By Destiny
Compelled
Fate's Intervention
Chosen Three
The Hidden Secrets Saga: The Complete Series

Kerrigan Chronicles
Stopping Time
A Passage of Time
Ticking Clock
Secrets in Time
Time in the City
Ultimate Future

Kerrigan Memoirs
Chronicles of Devon
Chronicles of Angel
Chronicles of Julian

Chronicles of Molly
Chronicles of Gabriel

Mending Magic Series
Lost Souls
Illusion of Power
Challenging the Dark
Castle of Power
Limits of Magic
Protectors of Light
Mending Magic Box Set Books #1-3

Omega Queen Series
Discipline
Bravery
Courage
Conquer
Strength
Validation
Approval
Blessing
Balance
Grievance
Enchanted
Gratified
Omega Queen - Box Set Books #1-3

Paranormal Huntress Series

Never Look Back
Coven Master
Alpha's Permission
Blood Bonding
Oracle of Nightmares
Shadows in the Night
Paranormal Huntress BOX SET

Prophecy Series
Only the Beginning
White Winter
Secrets of Destiny

Revamped Series
Hidden
Banished
Converted

Royal Factions
The Price For Peace
The Cost for Surviving
The Punishment For Deception
Faking Perfection
The Most Cherished
The Strength to Endure
Royal Factions Box Set Books #1-3

Royal Guard Series
Guardian
Paladin
Sentinel

The Chronicles of Kerrigan
Rae of Hope
Dark Nebula
House of Cards
Royal Tea
Under Fire
End in Sight
Hidden Darkness
Twisted Together
Mark of Fate
Strength & Power
Last One Standing
Rae of Light
The Chronicles of Kerrigan Box Set Books # 1 - 6

The Chronicles of Kerrigan: Gabriel
Living in the Past
Present For Today
Staring at the Future

The Chronicles of Kerrigan Prequel

Christmas Before the Magic
Question the Darkness
Into the Darkness
Fight the Darkness
Alone in the Darkness
Lost in Darkness
The Chronicles of Kerrigan Prequel Series Books #1-3

The Chronicles of Kerrigan Sequel
A Matter of Time
Time Piece
Second Chance
Glitch in Time
Our Time
Precious Time

The Hidden Secrets Saga
Seventh Mark (part 1 & 2)

The Kerrigan Kids
School of Potential
Myths & Magic
Kith & Kin
Playing With Power
Line of Ancestry
Descent of Hope
Illusion of Shadows
Frozen by the Future

Guilt Of My Past
Demise of Magic
Rise of The Prophecy
Deafened By The Past
The Kerrigan Kids Box Set Books #1-3

The Queen's Alpha Series
Eternal
Everlasting
Unceasing
Evermore
Forever
Boundless
Prophecy
Protected
Foretelling
Revelation
Betrayal
Resolved
The Queen's Alpha Box Set

The Senseless Series
Radium Halos - Part 1
Radium Halos - Part 2
Nonsense
Perception
The Senseless - Box Set Books #1-4

Standalone
Shadow of Doubt (Part 1 & 2)
Five Shades of Fantasy
Zwarte Nevel
Shadow of Doubt - Part 1
Shadow of Doubt - Part 2
Four and a Half Shades of Fantasy
Dream Fighter
What Creeps in the Night
Forest of the Forbidden
Arcane Forest: A Fantasy Anthology
The First Fantasy Box Set

Watch for more at www.wjmaybooks.com.

About the Author

About W.J. May

Welcome to USA TODAY BESTSELLING author W.J. May's Page! SIGN UP for W.J. May's Newsletter to find out about new releases, updates, cover reveals and even freebies! http://eepurl.com/97aYf

Website: http://www.wjmaybooks.com

Facebook: http://www.facebook.com/pages/Author-WJ-May-FAN-PAGE/141170442608149?ref=hl *Please feel free to connect with me and share your comments. I love connecting with my readers.* W.J. May grew up in the fruit belt of Ontario. Crazy-happy childhood, she always has had a vivid imagination and loads of energy. After her father passed away in 2008, from a six-year battle with cancer (which she still believes he won the fight against), she began to write again. A passion she'd loved for years, but realized life was too short to keep putting it off. She is a writer of Young Adult, Fantasy Fiction and where ever else her little muses take her.

Read more at www.wjmaybooks.com.